For Tom Moffatt,
a fellow Sherlockian
with every good wish

THE GAME IS AFOOT

Dubuque
5/31/88

THE GAME IS AFOOT

A Travel Guide to
the England of Sherlock Holmes

David L. Hammer

GASOGENE PRESS, Ltd.

Box 1041
Dubuque, IA 52004-1041

Jean R. Starr, *Managing Editor*
Jack Tracy, *Maps*
Mary Jane Gormley, *Calligraphy*
Thomson-Shore, *Printing and Binding*

Library of Congress Catalogue Number: 81–82194

ISBN 0–938501–03–8

Printed in the United States of America

10 9 8 7 6 5 4 3 2

It was on a bitterly cold night and frosty morning, towards the end of the winter of '97, that I was awakened by a tugging at my shoulder. It was Holmes. The candle in his hand shown upon his eager, stooping face, and told me at a glance that something was amiss.

"Come, Watson, come!" he cried. "The game is afoot. Not a word! Into your clothes and come!"

–*The Abbey Grange*

To Audrey—
The comrade of my journeys
who is the companion of my years

Preface

THERE is a certain sense of illogic in completing a book and then writing the preface. For a subject such as this, perhaps the more ancient prefatory apologia is indicated, as these are very special people who are being written about—fictional people who have by a famous Victorian writer's magic alchemy surmounted their literary dimensions and become wholly real, or, if you prefer, really whole. One can only write about their places and their times in the full recognition that no description could equal the Watsonian care and vigor in drawing a background.

There are too many books about Holmes and Watson, and the evidence of this is the plethora of novels featuring what were subsidiary characters in the saga together with literary criticism being analyzed by further literary criticism. The need is to put the Canon to the acid test—to return to the original source and determine its historicity. It is this enthusiast's contention that, amid the abundance of Sherlockian literature, the emphasis should be on scholarship and not on sensationalism. The sources themselves should be pursued.

This particular quest has taken this fortunate writer through many English counties and into homes, cottages, and castles alike. It is a tribute to "our blessed Sherlock" that his name has been a sufficient talisman to cause strangers to open their doors and permit an aging devotee to trespass over their grounds and intrude upon their privacy.

It has been my great and good fortune to have seen most of the possible sites in the course of the research for this book, a thoroughly delightful experience and one which has made my wife a believer.

There are few residences located with any simple certainty in the Canon. This fact has been regarded by some as significant evidence that they are stories only, made up out of whole cloth by a brilliant and inventive author. The difficulty in accepting that explanation lies in the enormous differences separating our age from that era in which Holmes investigated and Watson wrote. Two world wars and a coarsening of manners inhibit our understanding of a gentler and generally more hopeful time.

To the Victorians, a good reputation, whether deserved or not, was vitally important. They did not disclose private matters because of respect for the privacy of the other inhabitants of that increasingly crowded little island. For example, a common enough literary device of those days was to use only the first letters of names and places when discussing essentially private matters of some public interest. Dr. Watson did not subscribe to what we now regard as a foolish, but pleasant, conceit; he substituted names similar in spirit, juggled dates, and not only was vague as to locations but almost invariably provided different place names. This practice was in accord with the ethical character of the good doctor and undoubtedly had its genesis in his medical scruples. Still, his integrity, or perhaps his ingenuity, required him to leave something of the names, whether proper or place, in his substitutions. Some are rather obvious, and others are sufficiently subtle to retain only a kindred spirit.

What follows is an attempt to locate and identify the geographical verities of the Canon, a literary pilgrimage sufficient unto itself for any Holmesian, but yielding rather surprising results.

DAVID L. HAMMER

March 7, 1981
Dubuque, Iowa

Sir Arthur Conan Doyle's house in the London suburb of South Norwood—"modest but comfortable, isolated and yet one of a row"—where he lived 1891-94 and where the *Adventures* and *Memoirs* of Sherlock Holmes were written. At the time this photograph was taken, the house was undergoing renovation. The round plaque commemorating Doyle's residence can be seen at the right.

Contents

At right: The former
New Scotland Yard,
for eighty years the
headquarters of London's
Metropolitan Police

London: City Centre

I. Sherlock Holmes's London Residences

Baker Street

It was an overcast and appropriately dismal day to begin the physical search of Baker Street. London's Clean Air Act has forever banished the fogs of Dickens and Doyle, and a rainy day is the only substitute. Fortunately, London weather provides this, but the rains are showers and seldom last more than a few minutes. It is no accident that Londoners daily carry umbrellas.

Baker Street is now predominantly commercial, as it was beginning to be in Sherlock Holmes's day. There are no serious reminders of the immortal detective in the area, and the only Holmesian note is the Sherlock Holmes Cinema, but it is an area which Holmes would still recognize. Aside from the east side of Baker Street north of the Marylebone Road and an occasional obtrusive modern building such as the Abbey Bank building at the 221B site, structurally it is much as it was a hundred years ago. The buildings are preponderantly old, dull-red-brick, three-story structures with the street (or ground) floor relegated to stores and the remaining two stories to apartments. Ground floors were let to merchants in Holmes's day, a not uncommon practice in cities since Roman times. If there were fewer stores in the 1880s and 1890s, to recapture the architectural view then go to the northerly end of Baker Street, by Regent's Park where Park Road intersects.

The buildings on Park Road are virtually identical to those on Baker Street but have fewer stores.

The area remaining closest in appearance to that of Holmes's day is the quarter from Park Road south to Melcome Street, with most of the houses of that period being on the west side of the street. Any of these houses could physically pass as the Victorian lair of Holmes and Watson.

It had been good to capture the flavor of Baker Street, and it was time to return to the hotel. Everyone has his own special London hotel, and mine is Durrants. It is a fine old Georgian hostelry, four stories in height, situated immedi-diately behind the Wallace Collection, which is on the north side of Manchester Square. The Durrants is one of those small hotels which dot England and which make traveling there a delight, having furnished bed and breakfast to at least six generations of visitors. On chilly evenings, there is a fire in the grate of the tap room, a small and comfortable room for pre-dinner libations to whatever household gods inhabit Durrants. It is not an aristocratic hostelry—what is left of the aristocracy, still a large number in Britain, prefer more subtly elaborate quarters. But Durrants is the gathering place for many from the country. It is a quiet family hotel, and a proud non-member of any chain. The drawing room has that funereal quiet the British relish, with the obligatory paneled walls of time-darkened old wood. Here and there are vases on stands and the usual hunting and Rowlandson's Dr. Syntax prints over-elaborately framed. The guests are pleasantly cosseted by that test of a comfortable hotel: entirely invisible or visibly unobtrusive servants. And of course, for the Holmesian, it is on George Street but at its union with Baker Street.

Relaxing there in warm comfort on a dampish September evening, with the vast bordering pile of the Wallace Collection

Baker Street today: looking southward from Blandford Street

looming against the lighted sky, I felt that this was the perfect prelude to a continuation the following day of the search for the Baker Street home of the Master. Sitting by the small coal fire, it occurred to me that there has probably been more research by Holmesians regarding the location of 221B Baker Street than on any other Sherlockian subject, which is an anomaly as it is one of the few locations in the Holmes Canon for which a specific address is given. My research during those winter evenings back home had satisfied me of the fact that during the entire period of Holmes's detective career there was no dwelling designated as 221B Baker Street. This much could be established. Indeed, it was not until 1930 that a building was designated as No. 221 Baker Street, when the houses on that street were renumbered. Appropriately enough, it was the year of Sir Arthur Conan Doyle's death. The Baker Street of Holmes's day was a very short street bounded by Portman Square on the south and York Place on the north, with Upper Baker Street beginning at the intersection of the Marylebone Road. It was the same street, but, as in too many European cities, different portions arbitrarily bore different names.

It is necessary for the traveler seeking that elusive residence to consider the various locations already proposed.

221B Baker Street. This was the house which became No. 221 Baker Street in 1930, when the entire length of the street was designated Baker Street. A. L. Shearn proposed this dwelling, but it is a difficult thing to grant Watson the

Baker Street as it appeared shortly after Holmes and Watson took up residence at the elusive 221B in 1881. The view is northward from Dorset Street.

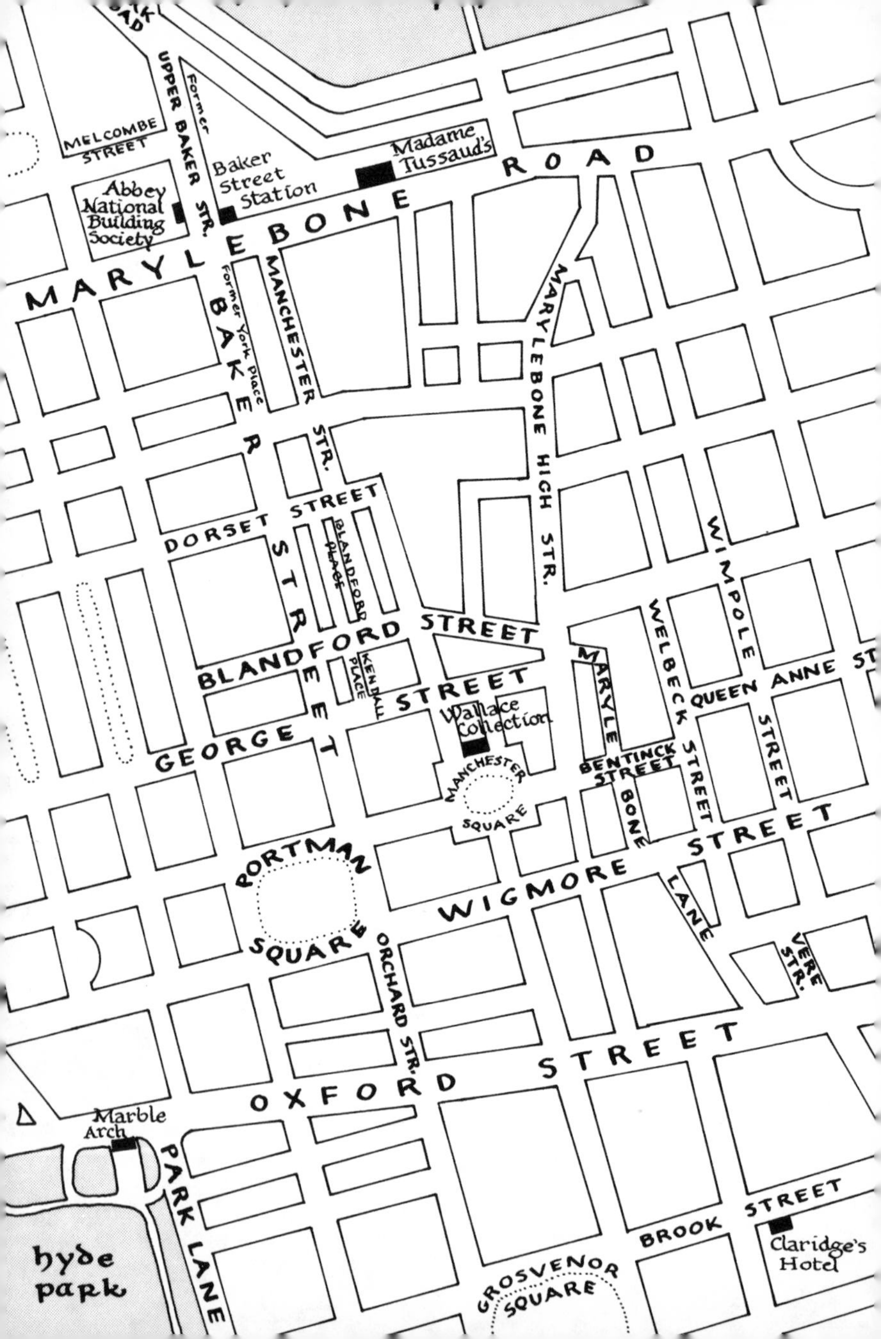

Former
UPPER BAKER STR.
MELCOMBE STREET
Abbey National Building Society
Baker Street Station
Madame Tussaud's
MARYLEBONE ROAD
Former York Place
BAKER STREET
MANCHESTER STR.
MARYLEBONE HIGH STR.
DORSET STREET
BLANDFORD PLACE
BLANDFORD STREET
KENDALL PLACE
GEORGE STREET
Wallace Collection
MANCHESTER SQUARE
MARYLEBONE LANE
BENTINCK STREET
WELBECK STREET
WIMPOLE STREET
QUEEN ANNE ST
PORTMAN SQUARE
WIGMORE STREET
ORCHARD STR.
VERE STR.
OXFORD STREET
Marble Arch
PARK LANE
hyde park
BROOK STREET
Claridge's Hotel
GROSVENOR SQUARE

prescience in 1887 to have anticipated a house designation fifty years in the future. There is not now a No. 221, the site being part of the headquarters of the Abbey National Building Society, a mortgage-lending institution famous for employing a secretary whose job it is to answer the thousands of letters arriving each year addressed to Sherlock Holmes.

49 Baker Street. This location was proposed by T. S. Blakeney on the basis of what he termed "reliable local authority," but it was destroyed in the London blitz.

59, 61, 63 Baker Street. Gavin Brend selected three likely locations, but believed No. 61 to have a slight preponderance of the evidence. Unfortunately, No. 61 has been torn down.

19 to 35 Baker Street. These are the selections of William S. Baring-Gould, based upon his location of Camden House, which according to the adventure of *The Empty House* stood opposite 221B Baker Street.

66 Baker Street. Originally designated by Vincent Starrett on the basis of an "occult sense of rightness," but his opinion was subsequently changed by the researches of Dr. Gray Chandler Briggs.

109 Baker Street. Ernest H. Short and James Edward Holroyd are responsible for this attribution.

111 Baker Street. The designation of Dr. Briggs, and concurred in by Vincent Starrett, was based upon the selection of No. 118 as Camden House.

31 Baker Street (formerly 72 Baker Street). This was the choice of Bernard Davies and has been destroyed, being now part of an office building.

There was near unanimity that 221B was located on the west side of Baker Street, although Baring-Gould, noting Watson's reference in *The Cardboard Box* to the August glare of the sunlight on the yellow brickwork of the house opposite

The headquarters of the Abbey National Building Society (with flag) occupy the present site of 221 Baker Street.

and postulating it was the morning sun, concludes that this would place 221 on the east side of the street. The activities of Holmes and Watson on that August day were reported with sufficient completeness to suggest that Watson's observation was not made in the morning, but, even assuming it was the morning sun, the specific reference was to the "glare of the sunlight," which could well have been the reflected glare from the direct sunlight on the fronts of the buildings on the west side of Baker Street. Thus, the Canon itself does not disprove the weight of the evidence that 221B was on the west side of the street.

The specific allusions in *The Empty House* to Blandford Street appear to establish the location of 221B as either 31 or 33 Baker Street, but this designation rests upon the assumption as to the location of the Empty House itself. If Charles

O. Merriman is correct in his identification of the Empty House as No. 34, then 221B would be No. 31.

Doyle's original holographic preliminary notes for *A Study in Scarlet* are the first reference to Holmes's Baker Street residence, and interestingly enough Doyle specifically referred to "221B *Upper* Baker Street," but the designation "Upper" was omitted in the printed work. This is of some significance. Until 1920, Upper Baker Street and Baker Street were different and distinct addresses, separated by a portion of the same street designated as "York Place." Indeed, the location of 221 Baker Street is on the west side of that portion of the present Baker Street which was formerly Upper Baker Street.

Upper Baker Street was a relatively short stretch of street, being that area between Marylebone Road on the south and Park Road on the north. Regent's Park was near its northern end. In Holmes's day, it consisted of Nos. 1 through 54,

Upper Baker Street as it appeared about the time of Holmes's retirement from his detective practice in 1903

Upper Baker Street, with Nos. 29 through 50 being on the west side of the street.

The most serious problem of Holmes's quarters being in Upper Baker Street lies in the meticulous directions given by Watson as to the location of the Empty House, which is categorically stated to be opposite 221B. As may be observed in the episode of *The Empty House,* there are problems with the Watsonian directions, but clearly the area in which he places that most celebrated vacant house is many blocks south from Upper Baker Street.

No search for 221B can be complete, however, without appropriate inquiry into the identity of the Empty House. April of the year 1894 marked Holmes's resurrection and his startling reunion with Watson. What Holmes later termed the Park Lane Mystery had brought them together at Marble Arch, situated at the northern corner of Hyde Park formed by the intersection of Park Lane and Oxford Street. It was a meeting which culminated in Watson, that old Afghan campaigner, fainting dead away in his study.

Holmes, who regarded his intended assassin, Colonel Sebastian Moran, as the second most dangerous man in London, had carefully prepared and baited a trap for the menacing and thoroughly evil big-game hunter. It was a ploy upon which he was later to expand in *The Mazarin Stone* with equal success. By a devious and circuitous night route, Holmes took Watson to a certain empty house, to be thereafter forever celebrated as *The Empty House,* which was opposite 221B Baker Street, there to await the arrival of Colonel Moran and his sinister air-gun.

Intricately linked with the search for 221B, then, is the search for the location of that Empty House. Several very specific designations are given: it was declared by Holmes to be called Camden House; it had a fanlight over the door; Holmes turned to his right from the hall into the front room; and the rear of the house was reached by turning "down a narrow passage" from Blandford Street.

Blandford Street runs east and west and intersects Baker Street at right angles. In 1894, there were mews parallel to Baker Street and extending north and south from Blandford Street, those extending to the north being Blandford Mews and those to the south Kendall Mews. What are mews? They are the alleys along which stables were located. In our time, they are still there, but many have long since been converted into rather expensive apartments. The mews east of and paralleling Baker Street have not been all converted, and many remain as garages, to which they were altered in the 1920s.

There are as many candidates for the Empty House as for 221B, and the most which can be said is that it remains a shadowy location.

Is there any evidence extrinsic to the Canon of a Holmes-Watson presence on Upper Baker Street? Or even Mrs. Hudson? The answer is no—not on Upper Baker Street nor Baker Street itself.* There are two sources of information—first, the annual London Post Office Directory, and second, the Register of Persons Entitled to Vote.

In preparation for the Baker Street examination in chief, I had gone to the Middlesex Record Office to check councilar voting records, London telephone books, and other extant

---

*One Louis Watson, a maker of artificial teeth, engaged quarters at No. 30 Upper Baker Street in 1900, but this obviously is the wrong Watson.

The entrance to Kendall Mews (now called Kendall Place), looking to the southward off Blandford Street

records of the 1870s, '80s and '90s. The Record Office is in Whitehall, near the Treasury, reachable from it through a rabbit warren of streets. It is a particularly ugly Victorian building whose dusty interior possesses that distinctively archival odor of disintegrating yellowed paper and the equally distinctive silence punctuated only by researchers turning endless brittle pages and moving in diseased chairs. It is almost as if the ordained silence were an effort to hold back time and its agent, decay. It seemed somehow an appropriate setting for Holmes research.

While women were not wholly enfranchised in Victorian England, some female property holders could vote in county elections, although not for members of Parliament, but no Mrs. Hudson is listed as eligible, nor does she appear in the

Kendall Place mews: one of these may be the famous Camden House, despite the absence of a back garden. These are the same buildings shown on p. 16.

London Post Office Directory. There is some information to be gleaned from records as to Upper Baker Street landladies of the time, but nothing definitive. There are several possibilities for the real Mrs. Hudson. Miss Emily Heather, who resided at No. 25 on the east side of the street, was in 1887 renting two first-floor rooms, two second-floor rooms and the third-floor front, furnished, to Mr. Martin John King Beecher for £335 yearly. On the west side of the street, Miss Deborah Sarah Marchant, who lived at No. 53, rented space on the second floor of No. 43 to Mr. Charles William Hallest for ten shillings per week.

Upper Baker Street had no dearth of flats to be rented. As early as 1880, Miss Sophia Pyman rented flats at No. 19, Mrs. E. H. Westbeare at No. 26, Mrs. Sarah Ennis at No. 36, Miss

Nicol at No. 42, and Alvah H. Axford at No. 47. Perhaps among these Victorian women may rest the elusive key to Mrs. Hudson and the location of the actual 221B, but for me the place was more interesting than the provenance, and ten minutes on Baker Street near Regent's Park was worth more than two hours in the Middlesex Record Office.

Montague Street

Thanks to the investigative efforts of Michael Harrison, there is no dispute about the location of Holmes's first London residence.

As Holmes confided to Watson in *The Musgrave Ritual,* when he first came to London he "had rooms in Montague Street, just round the corner from the British Museum." This is in the Bloomsbury area, east of the Museum, and it is substantially the same as it was in Holmes's day. Montague Street runs in a north-south direction between Russell Square on the north and Great Russell Street on the south. The British Museum is on the west side of the street, fronting on Great Russell Street, so that Holmes was accurate in his description, although there is an entrance on Montague Street. This is Bloomsbury, fabled in the early years of this century as the *avant garde* literary capital of London, just as a hundred years before it was the elegant residential quarter of the Metropolis. The houses which remain from Bloomsbury's early aristocratic period, and there are more than a few, are fine examples of the Georgian architectural style.

In keeping with his chariness about divulging personal matters, even to Watson, and then almost on a need-to-know basis, Holmes did not discuss the location of his Montague Street quarters. We are not without some information about them from outside the Canon, however. One of the finest Sherlockian scholars living today is Michael Harrison, a prolific and productive writer about Holmes and his world. He has developed some interesting information concerning the location of Holmes's quarters. By checking old volumes of the London Post Office Directory, he learned that a "Mrs. Holmes" had rented No. 26 Montague Street. The owner of the freehold was the Duchy of Bedford Estate, which he consulted, but the Duchy's records identified her no further, nor did the tax records, although he was able to determine that the lease was for seven years, commencing with the Michaelmas quarter in 1877.*

Across the street is the British Museum, which is not only a national but an international treasure. Aside from its many collections, its reading room has housed a variety of students ranging from the arch-communists Marx and Lenin to the also aggrieved Mr. Henry Baker of *The Blue Carbuncle* fame.

While the heavy fogs which once plagued Londoners and pleasured mystery writers have been abated, London, and all England, is subject to sudden showers, and there is a sort of grayness about the capital. Each provides a suitable ambience for a search for things Sherlockian, and both graced London the afternoon we explored the precincts of the Museum. This area is what the British would term a mixed bag. There are row houses around the immediate perimeter of the Museum, but beyond that there are the typical small antiquarian shops

---

*As reported in Harrison's *The World of Sherlock Holmes* (1974). In *The London of Sherlock Holmes* (1972), he gives the address as No. 24 Montague Street, but personal correspondence between Harrison and Gaslight publisher Jack Tracy confirms No. 26 as correct.

Montague Street. Holmes lived at No. 26, probably with his mother, during 1877–81.

which cluster around museums, the inevitable pubs and stores, as well as the nearby University of London. It is within two blocks (a distinctly non-British measurement) of New Oxford Street, one of the major commercial thoroughfares of London.

The Montague Street houses are row structures, part of a ducal development of the Georgian period. They are identical in height, four stories plus a basement. The entrances are all on the right, with fanlights above and two windows on the (English) ground or (American) first floor. The three floors above each have three windows across, with the windows on the upper two floors much smaller than on the first (American second) floor. The latter windows extend from the floor to the ceiling and front on a low iron balcony extending along the front of the house. The top three floors are of old, dark brick, with the ground (American first) floor being of white stone. Iron railings surround the light wells for the basement windows. The only individual variations are the curtains and the different colored doors, with the general impression being one of neatness and comfortable respectability. These houses are of the same type as existed in the Baker Street of Holmes's day and, indeed, are found throughout London in varying stages of care and disrepair.

As we walked along Montague Street, taking too many photographs, and turned left along Montague Place—at No. 23 of which, incidentally, Conan Doyle lived when he also first came to London—it required little imagination to relive the Holmes era. The British, who are necessarily a crowded race, living insularly and densely in their island, have developed, like their Japanese cultural cousins, a studied indifference to their immediate surroundings. In America, the taking of photographs on a street would occasion people stopping and looking and probably inquiring, but on a British street you are treated as not being there at all. As a result, photos in England are usually unencumbered with bystanders, and, as clothing styles date photographs, your Holmes pictures are unsullied by anachronism.

We had neither time nor invitation to see any interiors, so the houses remain to us somewhat sad and drab because of the uniformity of the exteriors. Still, it was the type of housing which Holmes, a man essentially uninterested in his surroundings, would prefer. Montague Street is a must.

Within the Temple precincts

II.
The Red-Headed League

WATSON'S ties to his old bachelor establishment, and to Holmes, were strong. Although he was living in Kensington on the morning of October 9th in 1890, or, if the reader credits the inconsistent reference to the two-month-old newspaper, on April 27th of the same year, he found his way back to Baker Street. Holmes was engrossed in the affairs of a client, Jabez Wilson, a pawnbroker of Saxe-Coburg Square whose narrative of the Red-Headed League presented Holmes with a satisfying "three pipe problem."

The putative League's headquarters was listed as 7 Pope's Court but later was referred to by the distraught Wilson as 4 Pope's Court.

There is not presently any Pope's Court off Fleet Street, but Michael Harrison has ascertained that such a court was once located between Bell Yard and Chancery Lane, which is now closed. This is the heart of legal London and is across the street from the Inner Temple, which is one of the chambers of barristers. It is also a place of study for barristers-to-be, as well as being next door to the Royal Courts of Justice. Among others, the Inner Temple housed the chambers of Godfrey Norton, husband of Irene Adler. The barristers, who are the English trial lawyers, swarm over this area with their wigs and black gowns, while the solicitors congregate less spectacularly on nearby Chancery Lane at the Law Society.

The Royal Courts building was built in the 1880s and

dedicated by Queen Victoria, but it was made to look distinctively medieval. The Temple is legitimately medieval, full of stone nooks and crannies. The gardens of both the Inner and Middle Temples extend southward to the Thames Embankment, and the grass is virtually manicured. If you want evidence that the English take the long view, when Audrey inquired of one of the gardeners how long it took to get grass like that, he advised, "Six hundred years."

Not far away, directly off Fleet Street, near Ludgate Circus, is Poppins Court, which forms a connection between Fleet Street and St. Bride Street. It has been identified as the original of Pope's Court by Charles O. Merriman of the Sherlock Holmes Society of London in his *Tourist Guide to the London of Sherlock Holmes.* European-fashion, different portions of the same street bear different names, the Strand becoming Fleet Street, then Ludgate Hill, and so on. Poppins Court is still there, only about a quarter of a mile from the Temple, and between the two are a number of fascinating small courts, including Wine Office Court, where the ancient Cheshire Cheese Inn continues, as it did for Dr. Johnson, to purvey food and drink. It is a pleasant place to break for lunch. The Poppins Court area is filled with small businesses, including some delightful antiquarian shops. Bride Lane, across the street, has a Christopher Wren church with a Roman London museum in its basement, a serendipitous discovery made as a result of the German blitz.

Holmes had considerably less difficulty in locating Saxe-Coburg Square, where dwelt Jabez Wilson, than those of us who seek for it later. This is not for want of clues. The Canon states:

> We travelled by the Underground as far as Aldersgate; and a short walk took us to Saxe-Coburg Square . . . a poky, little, shabby-genteel

place, where four lines of dingy two-storied brick houses looked out into a small railed-in enclosure, where a lawn of weedy grass and a few clumps of faded laurel-bushes made a hard fight against a smoke-laden and uncongenial atmosphere.

Wilson's establishment was a corner house, and it was there that Spaulding–Clay laconically answered Holmes's request for directions to the Strand: "Third right, fourth left."

Wine Office Court and the entrance to the Cheshire Cheese in Dr. Johnson's day. The warren of courts and alleys off Fleet Street has changed little in two centuries.

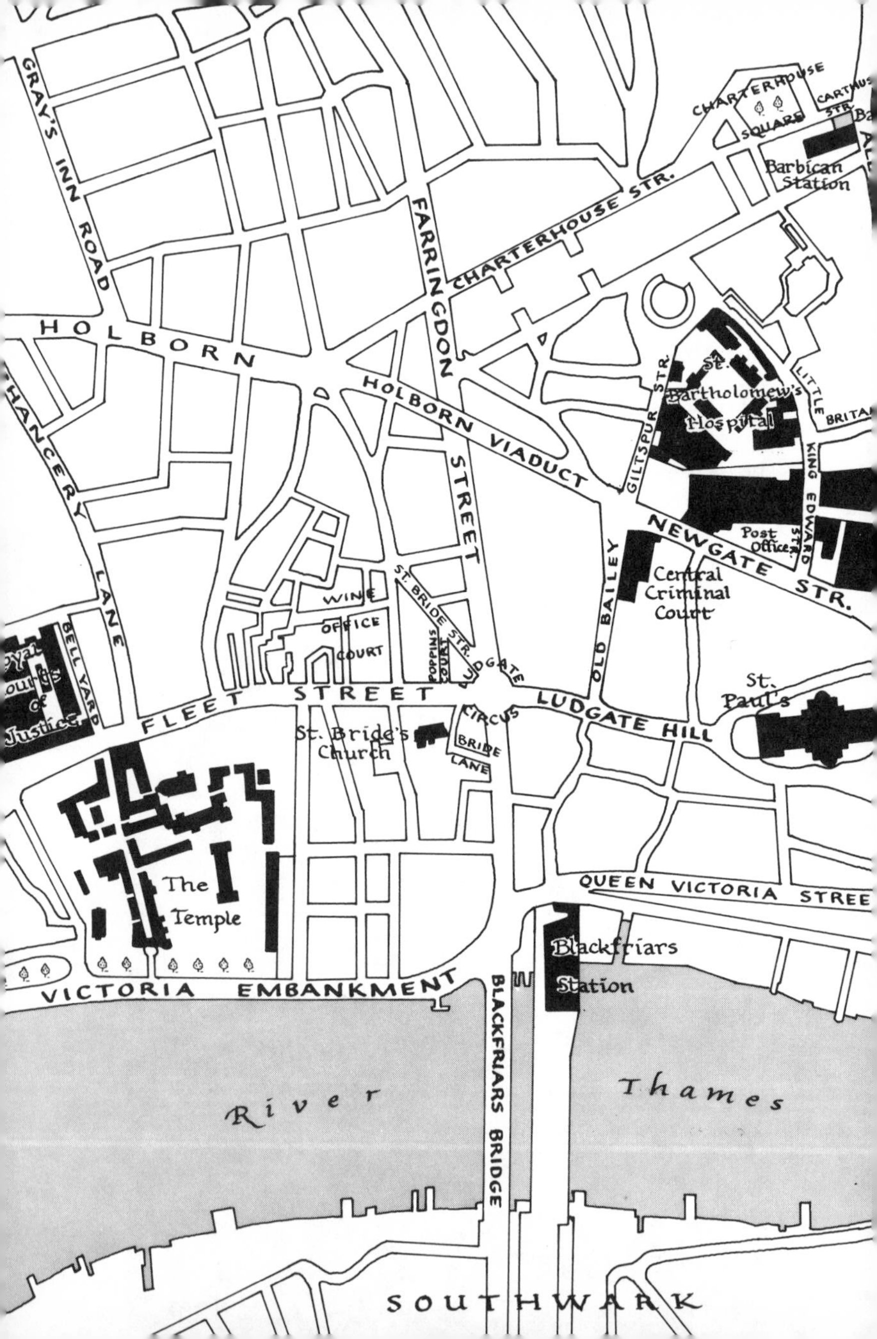

GRAY'S INN ROAD
CHARTERHOUSE
SQUARE
CARTHUS
STR.
Barbican
Station
CHARTERHOUSE STR.
FARRINGDON STREET
HOLBORN
HOLBORN VIADUCT
CHANCERY LANE
St.
Bartholomew's
Hospital
LITTLE
BRITA
GILTSPUR STR.
KING EDWARD STR.
NEWGATE STR.
Post
Office
OLD BAILEY
Central
Criminal
Court
WINE
OFFICE
COURT
ST. BRIDE STR.
POPPINS COURT
LUDGATE
BELL YARD
Courts
of
Justice
FLEET STREET
LUDGATE CIRCUS
LUDGATE HILL
St.
Paul's
St. Bride's
Church
BRIDE
LANE
QUEEN VICTORIA STREE
The
Temple
Blackfriars
Station
VICTORIA EMBANKMENT
BLACKFRIARS BRIDGE
River
Thames
SOUTHWARK

That same evening, Holmes and Watson left Baker Street with Peter (not Athelney) Jones of Scotland Yard and Mr. Merryweather, a director of the City and Suburban Bank, which was back-to-back with the Wilson establishment. The street in which the bank was situated was, in contrast to the "retired Saxe-Coburg Square," "one of the main arteries which conveyed the traffic of the City to the north and west."

They had traveled "through an endless labyrinth of gas-lit streets" until they "emerged into Farrington Street" and Holmes observed that they were close.

Saxe-Coburg Square is another one of Watson's geographical concealments, perhaps for the purpose of sparing the real Jabez Wilson embarrassment. There is no Saxe-Coburg Square, although, in view of the many intimate relationships between that ducal family and the British Royal house, it is surprising there is no square of that name.

Several squares have been suggested as the original. Michael Harrison proposed Charles Square, but it is some distance from Aldersgate Station, and he acknowledges the fact that it is Old Street Station which is by that Square. His explanation for the use of the farther station, that is, Aldersgate, as being a matter of Holmes's wariness, is questionable. While Charles Square meets certain of the physical requirements, including a bank on a busy thoroughfare by a quiet square, it does seem a bit more than "a short walk" from Aldersgate Station to Charles Square. It is about the same distance as the distance to the Strand, that is, from Chancery Lane to Charing Cross, but does not accord with the first Holmes-Clay colloquy. Holmes inquired of the renegade Clay at the Wilson establishment how to get to the Strand, which he would not have done at Charles Square as it is too obvious a ploy, being rather far from the Strand, nor would

Clay's directions, "Third right, fourth left," be even remotely accurate.

H. W. Bell proposed two locations many years ago: Charterhouse Square and Bridgewater Square, both of which are near to Aldersgate Station. Bell regarded Bridgewater Square as meeting the canonical descriptions, and it is quiet and square-shaped, although, if Clay's directions to the Strand were *reversed* in sequence, they would get a traveler very close to the Strand from Charterhouse Square. Farringdon Street (not Farrington as Watson erroneously spelled it) would be crossed going to either square.

After having studied the Canon and researched the locations, it was clear that as a preliminary hypothesis Aldersgate Station was a correct designation and our on-site investigation should begin there. The Monday morning we alighted at the station was satisfyingly close to the anniversary of the October 9 date upon which Holmes's adventure began. The weather was cold, with that particular bone-chilling dampness which makes fireplaces so welcome in Britain.

The Aldersgate Underground station from which Holmes and Watson emerged is now called the Barbican, and the station of their day has been demolished in the past few years. A characterless new structure has been erected on the foundations of the old, but the rail approaches are the same. Across the busy street, dismally modern apartments are springing up like excrescences from the blitzed earth.

We, as they, emerged on Aldersgate Street, which runs north and south and is the main traffic artery which Watson noted. Imagine our surprise upon reaching the street to see that, immediately north of the Underground station and separated only by a narrow alley, is a branch office of the National Westminster Bank, at 134 Aldersgate. Most buildings in England are what Americans would consider old, and, perhaps for the same reason that they prefer their statesmen old, they like their banks to have the solemnness of antiquity. The Aldersgate Branch of the National Westminster Bank was no exception to the rule. It was trimmed in dark wood, including the grilled tellers' cages, burnished bright where untold pounds and pence had passed. Malcolm Ogden, the assistant manager, was most considerate if a trifle bemused at our search, but the mention of Holmes opens most English

Aldersgate Street. The station, now rebuilt and called Barbican Station, is the low structure in the center of the photograph. Immediately next to it is the Aldersgate Street branch of the National Westminster Bank. Beyond the bank building, Carthusian Street leads into Charterhouse Square, the trees of which may be glimpsed above the roofs at left.

doors. He was kind enough to check the bank records, and we learned that the Aldersgate branch was opened at the same site in 1868 and was functioning at the time when Clay sought to remove the French bullion in the affair of the Red-Headed League.

The next step was to determine if there were a nearby square and if any buildings on the square abutted the bank. We hurried around the corner, just to the north, and we were on Carthusian Street, which intersects Aldersgate at a right angle. Carthusian Street is relatively short, and one hopes that it has seen better days. The south side of the street, after the corner building, which was quite respectable, although 1930s modern, consisted of a number of vacant shops on the ground, or first, floor and three floors of flats above. They were faded brick structures and had obviously been abused for some years, with peeling signs and the usual evidences of urban decay. They were posted with announcements of impending demolition.

Carthusian Street runs straight into Charterhouse Square. The square itself is somewhat irregularly shaped, with a small but pleasant wooded area in the middle. The buildings on the sides other than the south do not have the same aura of neglect. For the most part, they were originally built as upper-middle-class homes, probably late eighteenth century, four stories in height, brick with corner quoins in the same material. They are now offices rather than shops.

We particularly wished to see if the rear of the bank connected with any buildings on Charterhouse Square. It did. The rear of the bank clearly abutted the easternmost side of the house fronting on the south side of Carthusian Street, which forms the south side of Charterhouse Square.

Even skeptical Audrey acknowledged that the presence of

Charterhouse Square in better days, "with its blackened trees and garden, surrounded by ancient houses of the build of the [eighteenth] century, now slumbering like pensioners in the sunshine," as Thackeray wrote in *The Newcomes* in 1854. The invasion of commerce was well begun by Holmes's time, and in the 1890s Charterhouse Square was best known for the sporting equipment to be purchased here.

the bank made it a likely possibility that Saxe-Coburg Square could be Charterhouse Square. If it were, it would mean that the Jabez Wilson establishment would have to have been No. 3 Charterhouse Square or No. 10 Carthusian Street, each of which was the requisite vintage.

Returning to the north side of Carthusian Street to a pleasant Edwardian pub for English cider and an egg-and-veal-pie luncheon, it was time to consider the one remaining problem, that being Watson's reference to a physical and literal ninety-degree corner. On reflection, which is not an

The south side of Charterhouse Square at the entrance to Carthusian Street. In one of these buildings, now demolished, Jabez Wilson had his pawnshop.

essential function in a pub, it could with equal logic be an allusion to a corner of a square, such as here. In other words, the reference could have been to the Carthusian corner of the square.

The essential requirements linking Charterhouse Square with Saxe-Coburg Square were in place. It was close to the Underground station where Holmes and Watson alighted. Just around the corner there was a bank on a busy arterial thoroughfare and behind it a quiet square with buildings of the requisite age facing the square and abutting the rear of the bank. And finally, the directions given by John Clay, if reversed, would take a person from that very square to the

Strand. It seemed evident that H. W. Bell's suggested attribution was correct, and here it was that Wilson plodded, Clay plotted, and Holmes persevered.

* * *

A minor footnote to the matter of the Red-Headed League is found nearby, in King Edward Street, where, at No. 17, Jabez Wilson sought to find the elusive solicitor William Morris but found instead an artificial kneecap factory. As a street, it is short and undistinguished, connecting with Newgate Street on the south, and, after furnishing access to the General Post Office, it meets Little Britain Street and ends. Despite the drabness of King Edward Street and its continuation, Little Britain, it is not without a certain

One of the most striking views in London is this prospect of St. Paul's Cathedral, looking southward along King Edward Street, where Jabez Wilson vainly sought a solution to the conundrum of the Red-Headed League. St. Bartholomew's Hospital complex lies directly behind the photographer.

The main entrance to St. Bartholomew's Hospital

Sherlockian significance, for the St. Bartholomew's Hospital complex sits solemnly at the intersection of Little Britain and Giltspur Streets. More familiarly known as Bart's, St. Bartholomew's is a teaching hospital with firm antecedents in the twelfth century, when it was founded as a result of a promise of an ailing court official to do so if he recovered, and who was sufficiently ill to make such a promise and sufficiently honorable to remember.

Bart's is the typical English conglomerate of buildings of various periods and sizes connected one to another at various angles. The exterior would be still recognizable to Holmes and Watson, as probably would some of the interiors. They would, however, immediately miss the pervasive, late-nineteenth-century hospital smell of carbolic acid. Although it has changed considerably since that New Year's Day of 1881 when the most celebrated meeting in literature occurred, there is a plaque commemorating the occasion in the hospital precincts. If advance arrangements are made, it may be viewed. Bart's, recognizing its historic role in the saga, is tolerant of pilgrims.

III.
Piccadilly and Whitehall

THERE is in *The Illustrious Client* an interesting allusion to the Café Royal. The association is not culinary, but it is significant, for it was by the Regent Street entrance of the Café Royal that Holmes was brutally attacked by two thugs with sticks. His attackers were the minions of Baron Adelbert Gruner, the urbane collector and wife-killer.

The Café Royal is one of the most distinguished and fashionable restaurants in London, and has been so for well over a hundred years. Its two dining rooms, the Grill and Le Relais, both carry and merit the top Michelin English rating —five forks. It was founded in 1865 by an émigré Frenchman named Daniel Nicols, whose ever-present initial "N" is mistaken for that of Napoleon. The original entrance was on Glasshouse Street, but prosperity required an expansion westward to Regent Street, and it was through these two entrances that the thugs escaped after thrashing Holmes.

The present building is not the one existing at the time of the attack. The present quarters were constructed shortly after the First World War. The ambience and flavor of the original restaurant were perpetuated in the Grill Room, however, which has all the gold and mirrored opulence of the Second Empire. The baroque decor made it a favorite haunt of *fin de siècle* London, and Oscar Wilde was one of the habitués. It is what the English call pricey, but it is pleasant.

Located just off Piccadilly Circus, it shares a general

The Regent Street façade of the Café Royal today

location with the former Criterion Restaurant and Bar, which has no little Holmesian significance. It was at the Criterion Long Bar that Watson met young Stamford, his former colleague at Bart's, who introduced the good doctor to Sherlock Holmes. Named after the theatre next door and nicknamed "The Cri," it has fallen on hard times. It was recently a milk bar and is now a part of the Cockney Pride Tavern, an undistinguished public house. It faces Jermyn Street, but there is an extended corridor north to provide access to Piccadilly Circus, and one barroom with nineteenth-century murals is called the Criterion. I would speculate that the Long Bar was probably this long corridor. A plaque commemorating the meeting was placed on the north wall on the Piccadilly side by the Baritsu chapter of the Tokyo Baker Street Irregulars, but on our last trip to the site in 1979 it was no longer there, although its reappearance has since been reported.

Piccadilly Circus and the Criterion Long Bar as it was a century ago (above) and as it may be seen today (right) under the name of the Cockney Pride Tavern

Neville's Turkish Baths, in which *The Illustrious Client* opens, has long since ceased to minister to the aches and pains of the gentry. Its building remains, in the area between the Embankment tube station and Trafalgar Square, a small two-story structure with round tops on the ground floor windows which are vaguely Byzantine.

Craven Passage is literally that, a narrow defile permitting

The Sherlock Holmes, on Northumberland Street at its intersection with Northumberland Avenue, is the former Northumberland Hotel, where Sir Henry Baskerville stayed in *The Hound of the Baskervilles.* To the right of the hotel may be seen Craven Passage, leading to Craven Street, where Sir Henry's nemesis Stapleton lodged with his conscience-ridden wife. Leftward, Northumberland Avenue extends to Trafalgar Square; to the right, to the Thames Embankment. Immediately behind the photographer is Great Scotland Yard.

The famous reconstruction of the Baker Street sitting room at The Sherlock Holmes

no more than three persons abreast to go from Craven Street to Northumberland Street. Across that passage, on Northumberland Street where it intersects with Northumberland Avenue, is a site with Sherlockian associations, past and present, although not associated with *The Illustrious Client*. It was the Northumberland Hotel, and it was here that Sir Henry Baskerville stayed before going with Watson to Baskerville Hall and where he serially lost two boots. It is a well-maintained, four-story, red brick structure with white quoins and elaborate window embellishments, also in white, and a mansard roof. The ground floor boasts a famous public house—The Sherlock Holmes. Its walls are hung with mementos, and upstairs is a compressed Baker Street sitting room assembled for the Festival of Britain in 1951. The Whitbread Brewing Company owns and operates The Sherlock

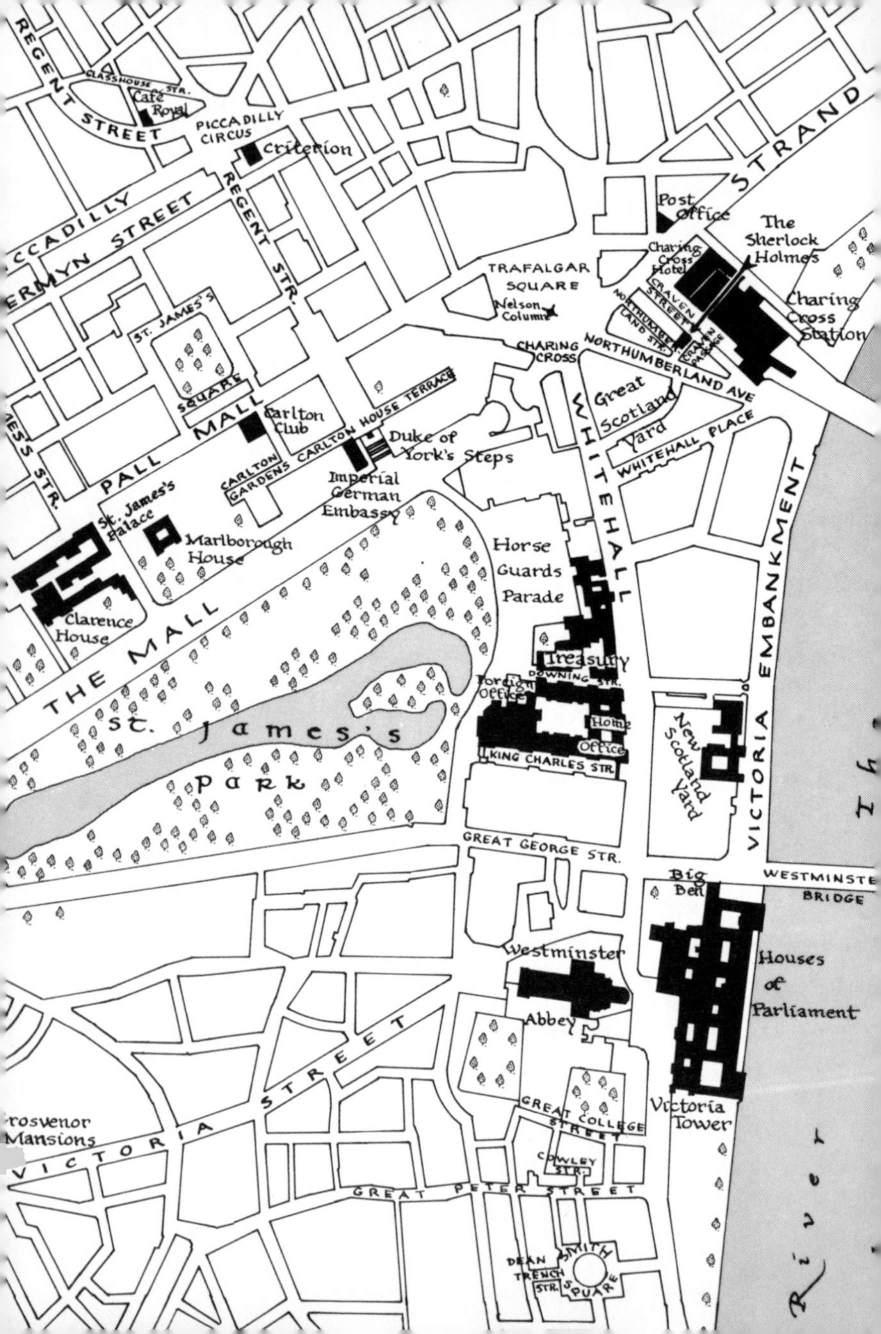
REGENT STREET
GLASSHOUSE STR.
Café Royal
PICCADILLY CIRCUS
Criterion
STRAND
Post Office
The Sherlock Holmes
Charing Cross Hotel
CRAVEN STREET
Charing Cross Station
TRAFALGAR SQUARE
Nelson Column
CHARING CROSS
NORTHUMBERLAND STR.
CRAVEN PASSAGE
NORTHUMBERLAND AVE
PICCADILLY
JERMYN STREET
REGENT STR.
ST. JAMES'S SQUARE
CARLTON HOUSE TERRACE
Great Scotland Yard
WHITEHALL PLACE
PALL MALL
Carlton Club
Duke of York's Steps
CARLTON GARDENS
Imperial German Embassy
WHITEHALL
VICTORIA EMBANKMENT
St. James's Palace
Marlborough House
Horse Guards Parade
Clarence House
THE MALL
Treasury
DOWNING STR.
Foreign Office
Home Office
KING CHARLES STR.
New Scotland Yard
St. James's Park
GREAT GEORGE STR.
Big Ben
WESTMINSTER BRIDGE
Westminster Abbey
Houses of Parliament
VICTORIA STREET
Grosvenor Mansions
GREAT COLLEGE STREET
Victoria Tower
COWLEY STR.
GREAT PETER STREET
DEAN TRENCH STR.
SMITH SQUARE
River Thames

Holmes. Many Whitehall types patronize it at luncheon, and in the evening, when the industry of government has shut down, a local and more relaxed group attends. Like all pub-keepers, the middle-aged couple who operate it are hospitable and convivial, and, as in all English pubs, tips for the barman are handled by the customers buying a drink for him.

Apart from the Sherlockian associations, it is a pleasant pub, and we regularly visit it. It is an excellent place from which to reconnoiter. Places touched with Sherlockian associations abound in this area but with only one exception are identifiable.

A short stroll down Northumberland Avenue will bring you to what was the site of New Scotland Yard from December 1890 until the mid-1970s. It is the large and ponderously Victorian building facing the Embankment at that point where Northumberland Avenue and Whitehall Place merge. Its first two stories are entirely faced with granite obligingly quarried by Dartmoor convicts, with red brick and stone appointments on the higher floors. Its predecessor was located

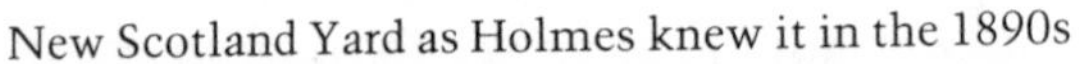
New Scotland Yard as Holmes knew it in the 1890s

Great Scotland Yard, headquarters of London's Metropolitan Police from 1829 until 1891

at No. 4 Whitehall Place, the rear portion of which, being the police station, was entered from Scotland Yard. The street had been so named ever since the 900s, when the Scottish kings or their ambassadors began staying there when they visited London. The original building housing the C.I.D. was soon outgrown; nearby structures were acquired, and, by the time of the building of New Scotland Yard, the complex housing the headquarters of the Metropolitan Police had become a rabbit warren of overcrowded, discontiguous buildings. This would have been the Yard as Holmes first knew it. This street is now called Great Scotland Yard, and you will pass its connection with Northumberland Avenue. The current, third, Scotland Yard has retained the name but has moved elsewhere into a concrete-and-glass highrise which suffices for our architecturally undistinguished age.

If you head back up Northumberland Avenue, away from the Embankment, you will come on one of the most celebrated squares in Britain—Trafalgar Square, whose center is dominated by the majestic Nelson column and its honor guard of pigeons, to neither of which any Sherlockian significance attaches.

The massive pile of fake Gothic on the east side of the square is Charing Cross Station, and above it is the Charing Cross Hotel. As railway travel afforded the most comfortable means of transportation in the Victorian era, elegance became quickly associated with it. Fine hotels were built in conjunction with stations, although usually not above them as was

Charing Cross Station and Hotel at the turn of the century

A nineteenth-century view down the Strand from Trafalgar Square. The building in the center housed the Charing Cross Post Office. Northumberland Avenue enters at the extreme right of the photo, Pall Mall behind the photographer.

done here in 1864, and railroad restaurants became, and some remain, centers of Continental cuisine.

It was the smoking room of the Charing Cross Hotel to which the credulous Hugo Oberstein was inveigled from abroad and captured. In the waiting room, apparently of the station, one Matthews—otherwise unidentified—struck Holmes with such force as to knock out a tooth. Holmes and Watson had used the station themselves on that "frosty morning towards the end of the winter of '97" when they departed here for the Abbey Grange at Marsham in Kent.

Across the Strand to the northeast was the Charing Cross Post Office. At a time before telephones were in general use, the telegraph messenger was frequently seen, and Holmes made liberal use of the wire. From this particular office, the distraught John Scott Eccles wired Holmes about his odd stay at Wisteria Lodge and Holmes himself sent a message to the gentlemanly Captain Crocker in the same Abbey Grange matter. The building remains, but it is now a bank.

At the northwest corner of Trafalgar Square is the entrance to Pall Mall. The clubland of London was and is in the St. James's area and is centered around Pall Mall, which Holmes knew well because of his brother Mycroft's membership in the Diogenes Club. Sir James Damery wrote to Holmes from his

"There is something forbidding about these huge, sombre, material monasteries, called clubs, solemn temples of the best masculine form, compounded of gentlemen and waiters, dignity and servility," wrote E. V. Lucas in *A Wanderer in London* (1906). "Women are the exception here. Pall Mall has no sweet shade."

club, the Carlton, on behalf of Holmes's Illustrious Client, and indeed that adventure has many West End associations and could serve as an aristocratic primer.

Parallel to Pall Mall and facing St. James's Park is Carlton House Terrace, around which great white stone mansions cluster with a disdainful mien. It is a very short street, even including its extension, Carlton Gardens, but its length is inverse to its importance. The opulent buildings were originally town houses, and they have been occupied by movers and shakers. Here lived Admiral Beatty of World

The opulent Carlton House Terrace had become dominated by foreign Embassies in the early years of the century. The York column, commemorating the popular Duke of York, second son of George III, which stands at the head of Waterloo Steps, may be seen at the extreme left. The building to its right is the former Imperial German Embassy.

War I prominence and Charles de Gaulle during the world war following. Two structures have a Holmesian connection: the town house of the Duke of Holdernesse of Priory School fame shared this prestigious address with the Imperial German Embassy, which had most unsatisfactory dealings with one Altamont. Both associations are tangential, as the Carlton House area was not the scene of any action. Baron Von Herling was stationed at the Embassy here, and it was that edifice to which he referred in *His Last Bow* when he advised Von Bork at his Essex villa that he would see him the

The York column and Waterloo Steps from St. James's Park. As can be seen, there is no "little door" onto the steps from the German Embassy—but the building on the opposite side of the steps does have just such a door, of which the third-person author of *His Last Bow* must have been thinking when he put those words into the mouth of Baron Von Herling.

next day when he put "that signal book through the little door on the Duke of York's Steps." The Wilhelmine German Embassy was the first building next to the steps on the west, and, while it is no longer an embassy, the building remains. Carlton House Terrace and Gardens parallel the Mall, which leads directly to Buckingham Palace and, being designated a Royal road, is literally red. Carlton House Terrace, somewhat higher than the Mall, is connected with it by the steps, which extend around the base of a high column supporting the statue of an eighteenth-century Duke of York.

Immediately west of Carlton Gardens, in an even more exclusive, indeed Royal, enclave, is Marlborough House. Here Edward VII, as the Prince of Wales, lived, and the group with which he surrounded himself came to be known disapprovingly as the Marlborough House Set. Marlborough House has an unprepossessing red brick exterior and now houses a center for Commonwealth studies. Clarence House, where the present Queen Mother lives, is also nearby.

At the southwestern corner of Trafalgar Square begins Whitehall, the nerve center of the British Government, and which, two world wars ago, was the seat of the mighty British Empire. It is also the place where Mycroft Holmes exercised his considerable talents as a generalist for the Government. Coming from Trafalgar Square, the Horse Guards Parade is on the right, across which Mycroft would have moved his indolent bulk from his quarters in Pall Mall to his Whitehall office. What remains of Whitehall Palace is on the left, and it was from one of the windows in the upper floor banqueting hall that Charles I walked to the headsman, a crime which even Holmes could not attribute to the improbable machina-

The view southward down Whitehall, still the center of the British Government, reveals the Big Ben tower of the Houses of Parliament at its far end. ►

STONEGUARD LTD

tions of his archfoe, Moriarty. Just beyond and going off to the right is the drab cul-de-sac called Downing Street. The Chancellor of the Exchequer lives at No. 11, and just beyond on the same side is No. 10, the official residence of the Prime Minister. When the likes of Eduardo Lucas threatened the Empire in *The Second Stain,* here dwelt Lord Bellinger, and across the street is the massive pile of the Foreign Office where the unhappy Rt. Hon. Trelawney Hope presided as Foreign Minister. No. 10 Downing Street, with its dark brick exterior, is a disappointment to visitors. The undistinguished front entrance looks as if it should be the rear entrance. It must be

Whitehall. The Government Office Building, at left, is where Mycroft Holmes occasionally *was* the British Government. To its immediate right, partly concealed by the war memorial, is the entrance to Downing Street.

remembered, however, that understatement is an English virtue.

Beyond the Tuscan-towered Foreign Office building, which also serves the Home and Commonwealth Offices, is the Treasury building, the south entrance of which faces Great George Street, which, under another name, traverses Westminster Bridge, a block away. St. James's Park and its elongated lake are to the west, one of those natural English gardens in the masterly landscape tradition of Capability Brown.

Between the north façade of the Treasury and the south wall of the Foreign Office is King Charles Street, which is reached by a few steps up at its open western end. It was down this street that Joseph Harrison scurried with the Naval Treaty which he had filched from the desk in the Foreign Office where Watson's school friend, Tadpole Phelps, was copying it. In the interests of clarification, Phelps furnished to Holmes a rough diagram in which King Charles Street is referred to simply as Charles Street, as it was indeed known until after the First World War. The diagram also shows Charles Street connecting at right angles with Whitehall, which a century ago it did. While there is not today such an intersection, it does not appear that this lack of connection is recent.

Diagonally southeast from the Treasury are the Houses of Parliament, that striking example of Neo-Gothic architecture built in the early days of Victoria and rebuilt after the Second World War because of extensive bomb damage. Tours may be arranged to see this complex of buildings which nestles by the Thames. Viewed from Lambeth, across the river, it seems to rise from the depths by some Merlin-like alchemy.

Westminster Abbey—The Abbey to the Britons—across

the street from Parliament, contains much of England's richest dust but is innocent of any canonical connection. Just south of here, though, according to *The Second Stain,* was the Eduardo Lucas residence, in the study of which that well-known amateur tenor and professional foreign agent was found stabbed to death. You will not find it at 16 Godolphin Street, as that street does not exist, but Watson places the house explicitly "between the river and the Abbey, almost in the shadow of the great Tower of the Houses of Parliament."

There was no street name akin to Godolphin Street in Westminster, which left the pleasant alternative of prowling the trapezoidal area between Westminster Abbey and the Thames in search of the proper site. As Parliament lies to the east of the Abbey, between it and the river, Watson's reference had to be to the area to the south, and the stated proximity of Lucas's "small but select mansion" to the Victoria Tower was a substantially delimiting factor which reduced the scope of the search. Mindful of Watson's description—"one of the old-fashioned and secluded rows of eighteenth-century houses" and specifically "a high, dingy, narrow-chested house, prim, formal, and solid, like the century which gave it birth"—we studied Great College Street, Cowley Street, Great Peter Street, and others, and finally, via Dean Trench Street, we passed into Smith Square. Along the north side of this square stood a whole phalanx of dark brick eighteenth-century houses—high, dingy, narrow-chested, prim, formal, and solid. And behind them loomed the great Victoria Tower of the Houses of Parliament, an occult confirmation of our choice.

It seemed to us very likely that in one of these several adjacent residences had dwelt Eduardo Lucas, and that it was here that Lady Hilda Trelawney Hope exchanged a sovereign's

In one of these fine old Georgian houses, "almost in the shadow of the great Tower of the Houses of Parliament," Eduardo Lucas of *The Second Stain* met his fate.

imprudent letter for her own indiscreet one and a deranged Mme. Fournaye stabbed her husband to the heart.

It is not surprising that there are so many Holmesian associations in the area radiating from Piccadilly Circus and Trafalgar Square, the two most famous squares in London. Oddly enough, many non-Holmesian activities have and do occur here. Until as recently as the second of our world wars, these were centers of empire, tangible symbols of the greatest of powers, possessing dominion over a fifth of the globe. The buildings of empire largely remain, for the British are a conservative lot, chary of change. Form is particularly important on a crowded island, and the English are masters of retaining form and replacing content. It is called tradition.

At right: Park Lane,
in the 1890s the most
prestigeous thoroughfare
in all of London

IV. Kensington: Of Poisons, Plans and Plots

SHERLOCK HOLMES was dying. Mrs. Hudson thought so and said so to Dr. Watson. The cautious Watson, visiting Baker Street during the second year of his marriage, opined only that the detective's eyes had fever brightness and that he appeared "very ill." Holmes offensively repulsed all Watson's offers of medical assistance and urged him to contact, not a medical man, but one Culverton Smith, who was a Sumatran planter then staying in London at 13 Lower Burke Street.

According to Watson, Lower Burke Street "proved to be a line of fine houses lying in the vague borderland between Notting Hill and Kensington. The particular one at which my cabman pulled up had an air of smug and demure respectability in its old-fashioned iron railings, its massive folding-door, and its shining brasswork."

Lower Burke Street is a Watsonian substitution for the real name of the street. He places it geographically between Notting Hill and Kensington, and this effectively delimits the area of consideration to that bounded by Notting Hill on the north, Kensington High Street on the south, and Holland Park and Kensington Gardens, respectively, to the west and east. Two streets within this area suggested themselves as surrogates for Lower Burke Street: Pitt Street and Peel Street.

William Pitt and Edmund Burke were contemporaries in

the House of Commons, although Burke never became Prime Minister. Burke, who was of Irish birth, and Sir Robert Peel, who was not, were not political contemporaries, but both were associated inextricably with Ireland. Peel was Secretary for Ireland and later effectively supported Catholic emancipation, although he was not personally committed to such a course. Later, in the matter of *The Six Napoleons,* Holmes would visit Pitt Street, where reporter Horace Harker resided, but that was many years in the future. As there is no reference in *The Six Napoleons* to Culverton Smith's earlier residence there, this would seem to mitigate against Pitt Street as the location of the Smith residence.

There is another reason. Peel Street is much closer to Notting Hill Gate, and thus could more easily fit the description of "the vague borderland between Notting Hill and Kensington." It is a relatively short street, extending east and west between Kensington Church Street on the east and Campden Hill Road on the west. So much for books and maps.

It was summer before we could explore Peel Street and environs, which are easily reached by the Underground to Notting Hill Gate. While Kensington Church Street consists today largely of antique stores, Peel Street from the middle of the block westerly has retained its residential flavor. It is much as it was in the late 1880s and early 1890s.

Our search was for a row of five houses, one of which had "smug and demure respectability," "iron railings," "a massive folding door" (double doors), and "stunning brasswork." On the south side of Peel Street, commencing at its westerly intersection with Campden Hill Road, is a row of five houses, with a very similar sixth. Of the integral five, the second from

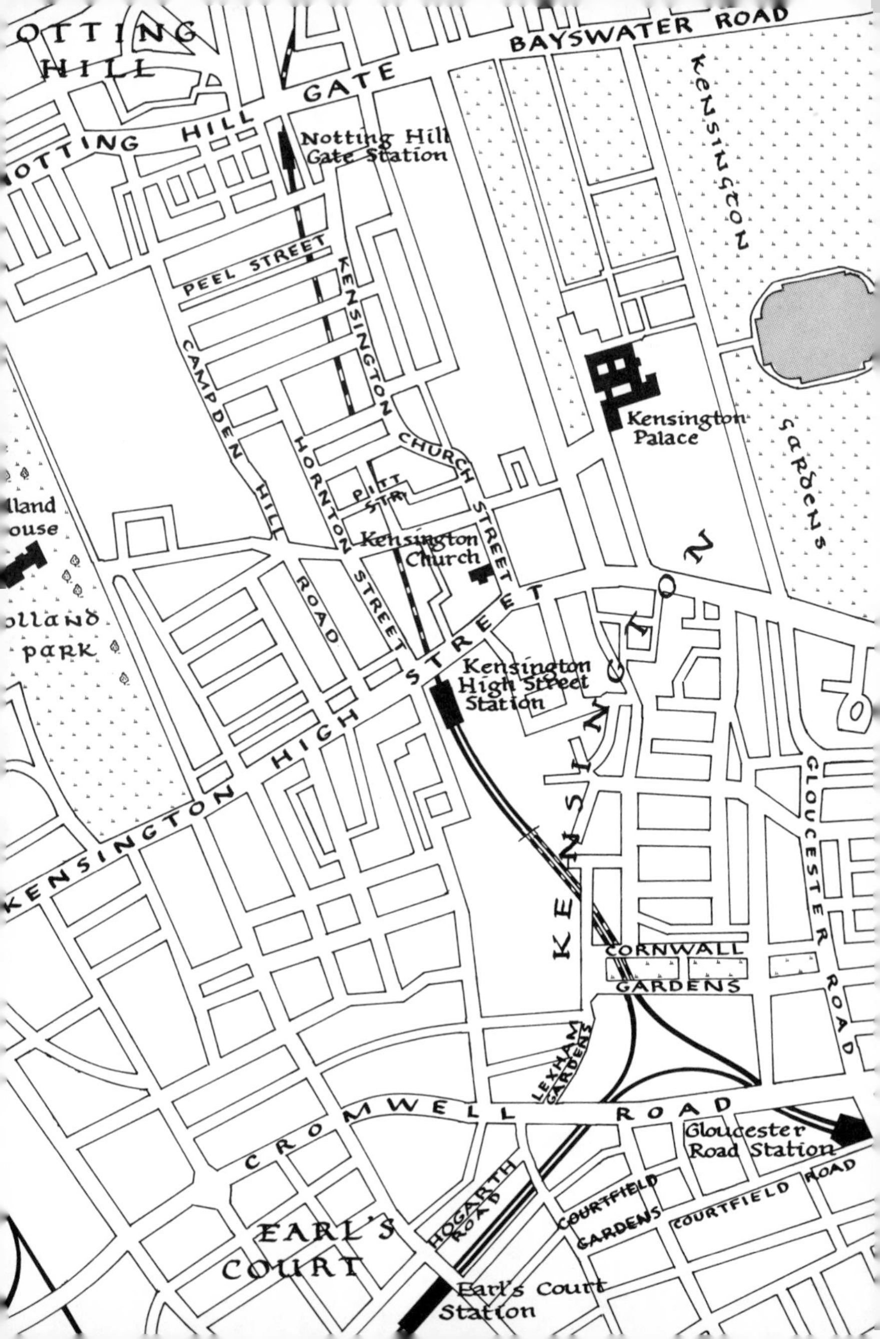

NOTTING HILL
BAYSWATER ROAD
NOTTING HILL GATE
Notting Hill Gate Station
KENSINGTON GARDENS
PEEL STREET
KENSINGTON CHURCH STREET
CAMPDEN HILL
HORNTON STREET
PITT STR
Kensington Palace
Kensington Church
Holland House
Holland Park
CAMPDEN HILL ROAD
KENSINGTON HIGH STREET
Kensington High Street Station
KENSINGTON
GLOUCESTER ROAD
CORNWALL GARDENS
LEXHAM GARDENS
CROMWELL ROAD
Gloucester Road Station
HOGARTH ROAD
COURTFIELD GARDENS
COURTFIELD ROAD
EARL'S COURT
Earl's Court Station

the end, now vaguely Georgian, has an iron railing and does exude an air of "smug and demure respectability." It is a two-story affair of white painted brick, with a bow window, a fanlight over its slightly recessed doorway, and boasting of shining brasswork.

It was only when our sapient publisher, Jack Tracy, read the typescript of this book that I learned that, in examining *The Dying Detective,* I had misread "fine" as "five" in Watson's description! But the attribution so possesses what Vincent Starrett called that "occult sense of rightness" that I still believe it to be accurate.

At all events, here was physical evidence confirming the Peel Street provisional attribution. There is a certain quiet elation which comes from developing a theory and empirically confirming it. Elation is always dangerous, and in this instance it dulled the edge of perception. We were walking along Kensington Church Street, and Audrey again mentioned the interesting antique stores. She was right. This was a preëminent antique quarter of London. It was difficult to suggest again that we should explore the Sherlockian site first, since we had done that. Perhaps they were interesting stores, but my particular antique interest span is shorter than hers.

I knew the rest of the day was shot when she spotted the shop of Dombey and Dombey. The Dickensian association intrigued her, and, observing on her way in that it was a shame it wasn't Dombey and Son, she disappeared. By late afternoon, we had learned much about the Messrs. Dombey, who, for the record, are brothers and purveyors of antique clocks. More significantly, we had acquired an ormolu-and-tortoise-shell presentation clock manufactured in Paris in

The white-painted house, second from right, was the lair of Culverton Smith during his murderous stay in London.

1854—a "chimer," as the younger Dombey characterized it. It now graces our living room mantel and still chimes, and each time it does my wallet twinges. Suffice it to say that I have my reasons for never forgetting Peel Street. There might also be a Dombey clock on the dining room mantel if I hadn't urged that we were going to be dining at a restaurant we both enjoyed, independent of its association with the adventure of *The Dying Detective.*

The menacing Culverton Smith agreed to Watson's entreaties to see Holmes, and while at Baker Street sought to accelerate the condition of the Dying Detective. Having successfully killed his kinsman, poor Victor Savage, he sought to dispatch Holmes by means of a similar bacterial poison.

With Smith's unwitting confession witnessed by a concealed Watson, Holmes, famished by his three-day fast and seeking to assuage his hunger, suggested that "something nutritious at Simpson's would not be out of place."

It is not necessary to feign mortal illness or successfully deal with an infamous Culverton Smith as a precondition for dinner at Simpson's. In Holmes's day, it was Simpson's Divan Tavern, and it is now called Simpson's-in-the-Strand and is owned and operated by the Savoy Hotel. Then, as now, it is at 103 Strand and continues to provide fine English fare. Michelin's 1978 edition for Great Britain and Ireland accords it a three-fork rating, which in our opinion is probably too conservative.

The "great saloon" of Simpson's Divan, the only restaurant at which Sherlock Holmes is known to have dined more than once, was famous for its roast beef and for its two great free-standing candelabra, by Holmes and Watson's day converted to gaslight.

Simpson's is comfortable rather than opulent, masculine rather than feminine, in decor; there is oak paneling rather than gilded plaster, and roast beef instead of *coq au vin*. The so-called *nouvelle cuisine* has been served here since long before it was introduced on the Continent—foods cooked in their own juices, and no sauces which overwhelm the natural taste of the food, except possibly English horseradish.

Here too, traditions are respected, the same ones as in Holmes's time—the roast beef trolley, the tip to the carver, the after-dinner port with Stilton cheese or walnuts.

Holmes and Watson continued to patronize Simpson's through the years. As late as September 1902, Holmes and Watson dined there during Holmes's bout with Baron Adelbert Gruner, that elegant collector of women, in Holmes's attempt to protect Violet de Merville from his malevolent machinations. During that case, Watson mentioned meeting Holmes by "appointment that evening at Simpson's," and later they "dined once more at our Strand restaurant." It is consolatory to think of Watson washing down his roast beef with his Beaune and Holmes savoring Dover sole with Montrachet, ceremoniously concluding one adventure and speculating upon the next.

* * *

A few blocks from Peel Street is another area with significant Sherlockian associations. Some years after the Culverton Smith matter, in 1900 if one accepts the ingenious Baring-Gould chronology, one Horace Harker, a reporter for the Central Press Syndicate, found a story on his own doorstep. It was not the presence of the murdered man which intrigued Holmes in *The Six Napoleons* but the singular eccentricity of a smashed bust of Napoleon I, the fourth one destroyed in two weeks. A curious Holmes had come to the Harker house, which Watson somewhat racily described as being "one of a row, all flat-chested, respectable and most unromantic dwellings," a description which may reveal more about Watson than the dwelling.

There is a Pitt Street, but there is no No. 131. The street lies in Kensington, a quarter not much changed from Harker's time, with lots of trees and slight hills and still fancied by middle- and upper-middle-class people.

Your own imagination should begin where Harker's adventure began, at the Kensington High Street Station. You will search fruitlessly for Harding Brothers' store, then "two doors" from the station, where Harker bought his Napoleonic bust, but the short walk uphill along Hornton Street to Pitt Street is very pleasant and would certainly have been the route of Harker and perhaps that of Holmes's cab.

H. W. Bell identifies the Harker residence as within a row of five dwellings, starting with No. 10, and selecting No. 14 as the most likely. These are all white, Regency-type houses which may meet the Watsonian characterization of flat-chested if the absence of bow windows is the test. Watson mentioned a railing, and such a railing does still exist. Holmes observed during his examination of the house that it was no mean feat to reach the ledge and open the window. No. 14, and all others in the same row, each possesses one window on the ground floor, the base of which is about three feet above the ground.

No. 13, across the street, possesses a much higher front window, which would furnish justification for Holmes's

Pitt Street: One of this row of Regency dwellings was the home of reporter Horace Harker, upon whose doorstep Pietro Venucci was murdered by the villainous Beppo.

assertion, but it does boast a two-story bow window, which is perhaps too bosomy for Watson.

The Harker bust had been removed from the premises and smashed to pieces in the front garden of an unidentified house around the corner in Campden House Road, which has long been renamed Hornton Street, the same thoroughfare along which we approached Pitt Street.

* * *

It was to Goldini's Restaurant on Gloucester Road in Kensington that Watson was summoned to join Holmes with "a jemmy, a dark lantern, a chisel, and a revolver"—"nice equipment for a respectable citizen to carry through the dim, fog-draped streets," the good doctor observed. Without demur, however, he promptly arrived with the gear stowed in his overcoat, finding it easier to locate Goldini's than for us today.

The object of the housebreaking tools was the home of Hugo Oberstein at 13 Caulfield Gardens. Oberstein was then one of London's resident crop of spies and was reasonably believed to be the person who had dispatched young Cadogan West in the affair of *The Bruce-Partington Plans.*

Caulfield Gardens has been described by Watson as "one of those lines of flat-faced, pillared, and porticoed houses which are so prominent a product of the middle Victorian epoch in the West End." By Holmes's estimate, it was a half-mile from Goldini's to Oberstein's house, and we know from the Canon that the rear of the house was contiguous to the open tracks of the Underground which served Gloucester Road Station, and further that the tops of the trains were less than four feet below at least one Oberstein rear window ledge. An additional clue as to its location is that on Holmes's second burglary of Oberstein's home he and Watson met Lestrade outside the Gloucester Road Station. The "massive" front door was quickly and professionally dismissed by Holmes as too difficult and too public for his attention, so an entry was forced through a door in the service areaway below the front door.

Such then is the extent of the description of the only house which Holmes did not scruple to burgle twice. There were, however, conclusions about the dwelling which could properly be drawn from outside the Canon. It was an upper-middle-class residence in what, at least then, was regarded as an upper-middle-class neighborhood. Watson's reference to the West End is not wholly geographical and is the term denoting an upper-middle-class and aristocratic life which was centered in the west of London. The presence of rail lines hard by houses was not regarded in the middle years of the nineteenth century as a negative fact. Stereotypes change, and living by the tracks was, both in England and America, not a social sin; indeed, many mansions were deliberately built near railroad tracks. Trains were the space-age vehicles of their day and represented the most significant forward development in transportation in centuries. Imagine—for thousands of years until rails arrived, the fastest speed on earth had been a horse's gallop, and then suddenly passengers could be hurtled along at speeds in excess of forty miles an hour.

The name Caulfield Gardens is another Watsonian substitution. The only reason for it would be habit, as there could be no reason to disguise the residence of a convicted spy. The location is rich in attributions: Christopher Morley believed the original was Courtfield Road or Courtfield Gardens, Michael Harrison reckoned it to be Cornwall Gardens, and both Bernard Davies and D. Martin Dakin held to Hogarth Road.

The place to begin is where Holmes and Watson met Lestrade, at the Gloucester Road Station. The station is still there, on Gloucester Road where it intersects with Courtfield Road. It is easily reached from High Street Station, if you have done Pitt Street, and is in fact the next station; indeed, in traveling between those two stations you will pass Cornwall Gardens, one of the proposed sites of Oberstein's house.

Courtfield Road extends southwest from Gloucester

Although a satisfactory identification has yet to be made, Hogarth Road remains the best likelihood for the location of spy Hugo Oberstein's house. ►

Station and becomes the south side of Courtfield Gardens, which actually form an odd-shaped square. This is a very pleasant enclave, with well-maintained old row dwellings from the middle-Victorian period. It was a late spring day when I wandered there, with an occasional quick sweeping of English rain adding a certain Holmesian ambience. These homes were porticoed with pillars, possessed a flat aspect, and each had a servants' entrance in the sub-street level and lacked nothing except for rearward open Underground tracks. It is a significant omission.

Hogarth Road is only three streets away and also consists of middle-Victorian row houses with pillared porticoes, tradesmen's entrances below the street, but, unfortunately, also bow windows. While the Hogarth Street houses still have an architectural aura of solid respectability, they are far less elaborate than the Courtfield Gardens houses. The most significant attribute of the Hogarth houses is the presence of the open Underground lines in their rear, but all those backs which could be viewed were too far away from the railroad cut to permit any body to be deposited on a train top. The street itself is much closer to the Earl's Court Underground station and is in the area more commonly denominated Earl's Court than Kensington. Moreover, Hogarth Street does not have the rich ambience which would have sheltered a spy back in times when that craft did not require concealment.

Michael Harrison, whose opinions as to Holmesian locations should not be lightly disregarded, has opined that Cornwall Gardens is the real counterpart of Caulfield Gardens. It was a year or two after examining Courtfield Gardens and Hogarth Road before I could visit Cornwall Gardens, but I did so on a Saturday in June, an uncharacteristically sweltering afternoon when Londoners carried their coats in dismay.

Cornwall Gardens is still a pleasant place, with a long and narrow private park in the center and white porticoed row houses on both sides. It has come down in the social scale—the houses have been broken up into small flats, and there was an unusual number of sale signs. The London maps show a portion of the open Underground from Earl's Court crossing the southwestern end of Cornwall Gardens, but the on-site investigation revealed that that is not accurate. The houses along the east side of Lexham Gardens, which adjoins Cornwall Gardens, do have rear yards abutting an open Underground cut, but the houses themselves are not close enough to the tracks to meet the requirements of the Oberstein house.

Unless some researcher can establish that at the time of *The Bruce-Partington Plans* there was an open cut along the western end of Cornwall Gardens, it must be eliminated as a possibility. Hogarth Road, although not as ornate as the other candidates, must remain the most likely possibility because of the open Underground track hard by the residences there.

V. Hyde Park

IT was not unnatural, given the wholesale importation of American heiresses by the impoverished British nobility, that sooner or later Holmes would become involved in what one society paper called "free trade" in the marriage market. By Watson's account, *The Noble Bachelor* commenced on an autumn afternoon of 1887, shortly before his marriage, and its beginning provides one of those delightful vignettes which are among the comforts particularly enjoyed by fireside readers.

> I had remained indoors all day, for the weather had taken a sudden turn to rain, with high autumnal winds, and the Jezail bullet which I had brought back in one of my limbs as a relic of my Afghan campaign throbbed with dull persistence. With my body in one easy chair and my legs upon another, I had surrounded myself with a cloud of newspapers until at last, saturated with the news of the day, I tossed them all aside and lay listless . . .

At 4:00 on that rainswept afternoon, Lord Robert St. Simon, the second son of the Duke of Balmoral, graced the Baker Street quarters with his aristocratic mien and patrician disdain. Lord Robert was missing his bride, not a common occurrence in his exalted circles, particularly as the bride had vanished during the wedding breakfast, an embarrassment which caused him considerable well-bred dismay.

The distressed bridegroom had an apartment at Grosvenor Mansions, which was and is on Victoria Street, at its intersection with Palace Street. It is in the Westminster section of London, rather closer to the royal stables than to Buckingham Palace, but acceptably near to the latter. W. S. Baring-Gould's researches reveal that construction was begun in 1858 but remained unfinished for many years, and that after its

Grosvenor Mansions, once the exclusive address of the likes of Lord Robert St. Simon, has come down considerably in the world.

completion the seven-story building consisted of luxury apartments. It is now largely used for offices and stores and is not really worth a look.

The bride and her father, Hatty and Aloysius Doran, had taken a "furnished house at Lancaster Gate," which would be on Bayswater Road. It was from the dining room of these premises, during the wedding breakfast, that the new Lady Robert St. Simon saw her American husband, long believed dead, motion to her from the park across the street. This would be Hyde Park, and this quarter was then and continues to the present to be among the finest residential areas in London.

The upper-class Victorians were keen horsemen and -women, and horses dominated their society, whether at the races at Epsom Downs and Newmarket, fox hunting on their estates, driving fours-in-hand, taking carriage rides, or riding daily in Hyde Park. The ladies participated in the rides in the Park, both on horseback and in elegant carriages, as when Irene Adler rode out "as usual" on the afternoon of her own wedding. Particular hours of the day were regarded as appropriate times to appear, and much criticism was leveled at the presence of the demimondaines in their rather garish finery.

Massive mansions rose along Park Lane and Bayswater Road during and after the 1860s. Galsworthy's Forsytes were placed here, and many of Oppenheim's heroes resided along the Park, like elegant frogs around a pond. To a Londoner of the last half of the nineteenth century, *the* Park was Hyde Park and the "Hyde" was superfluous. Aloysius Doran was well advised to greet the London season of May to July there, particularly if he sought an aristocratic alliance, and, if

"Hyde Park has still about it something of Arcadia," wrote Disraeli. "There are woods and waters, and the occasional illusion of an illimitable distance of sylvan joyance."

ultimately he lacked a lord as a son-in-law, his daughter was at least—and at last—reunited with her husband. No Victorian novelist could provide an ending more appropriate to the time.

What was termed the Park Lane Mystery occurred in the same region. The Honourable Ronald Adair, second son of the Earl of Maynooth, was shot dead in his locked room in his family's mansion at 427 Park Lane by a soft-nosed bullet. The absence of forced entry or of any weapon was profoundly mystifying if one did not know about Von Herder's celebrated air-gun and the proclivities of Colonel Sebastian Moran, late of one of Her Majesty's Indian regiments.

We were in London for a barristers' conference, and arrangements were made for us to stay at the Royal Lancaster, which is on the north side of Hyde Park and not surprisingly at Lancaster Gate. The street along the north side of the Park, from Park Lane west, is Bayswater Road. The long block to the east of the hotel has wholly retained its residential character, although by its height the Royal Lancaster dominates the neighborhood. The mansions were apparently built, all at the same time, as an elegant row development. They are of white stone, five stories in height, with porticoes and balustrades. Theirs is a restrained opulence, and some of them are now apartments. Any one of these mansions could have been the scene of that memorable wedding breakfast.

Park Lane, once the most fashionable of all London addresses, at the east end of Hyde Park, has suffered enormous commercial encroachments since 1894. The Grosvenor Hotel and other institutions have replaced most of the elegant mansions of Holmes's day. Fortunately, some business establishments have retained their façades intact, and there remain a sprinkling of exteriors sufficient to afford the flavor of that earlier time when Holmes relentlessly pursued the Colonel and his insidious air-gun. No. 128, and Nos. 94 through 99, Park Lane are evocative of that era. No. 427, the Adair mansion, would have been much like them, but there is no No. 427.

Here and there, Park Lane's former elegance peers out from amid the highrise hotels and commercial establishments. ►

It is not inappropriate that crime flourished here in Holmes's era, for nearby, at the intersection formed by Park Lane and the Bayswater Road, that intersection now called Marble Arch, is the site of Tyburn Tree, where public hangings took place until 1759, even after the tree itself had been replaced by a gibbet. This is the same corner at which Watson bumped into a certain elderly, hunchbacked bibliophile, and each time I passed there I looked for him too.

At right: The Logs, on the border of Hampstead Heath, long identified as Appledore Towers

London:
The Suburbs

VI. Hampstead and Mr. Milverton

EACH READER of the Canon has his own favorite malefactor, and many of us frankly never developed Holmes's enthusiasm for Professor Moriarty. One of my favorites has always been Charles Augustus Milverton, the Pickwickian-appearing blackmailer with the reptilian eyes.

Milverton lived in elegant comfort in his villa, Appledore Towers, in Hampstead, a northern London suburb. The villa is particularly significant as it was burgled by Holmes, with Watson's assistance, Milverton having bested Holmes when the latter attempted battery. The dénouement of this dramatic adventure begins on one of those Baker Street evenings which delight the soul. It was January 14, 1899, "a wild tempestuous evening, when the wind screamed and rattled against the windows." After a cold supper, Holmes and Watson donned evening clothes and, with concealed face masks, a dark lantern, and a housebreaking kit, set out to burgle Appledore Towers to retrieve Lady Eva Brackwell's compromising documents from Milverton's study safe.

Their route is recorded with unusual and exemplary exactitude—a hansom cab ride from Oxford Street to Church Row in Hampstead, a walk "along the edge of the heath" to the gate of Appledore Towers, a big house set within its own grounds with a tiled veranda along one side.

After the successful burglary and the witnessing of the timely death of the nefarious Milverton, they scaled the six-foot wall and escaped "across the huge expanse of Hampstead Heath," running some two miles and eluding their pursuers.

Baring-Gould had stated in *The Annotated Sherlock Holmes* that Humphrey Morton and the Milvertonians of Hampstead had identified Appledore Towers as The Logs, and included a rather vague picture of it, but that work was several years old and we could not be sure that the house was still there.

We knew from a previous visit that Hampstead was still a very fashionable suburb, as it had been when Keats lived there and wrote his *Ode to a Nightingale.* The Heath is one of those vast natural parks which were the English contribution to landscape gardening. The British cherish their walks, usually with dog and walking stick, and such an excursion at Hampstead Heath is a Sunday institution for many Londoners.

Our exploration of the habitat of the miscreant Holmes

On Hampstead Heath

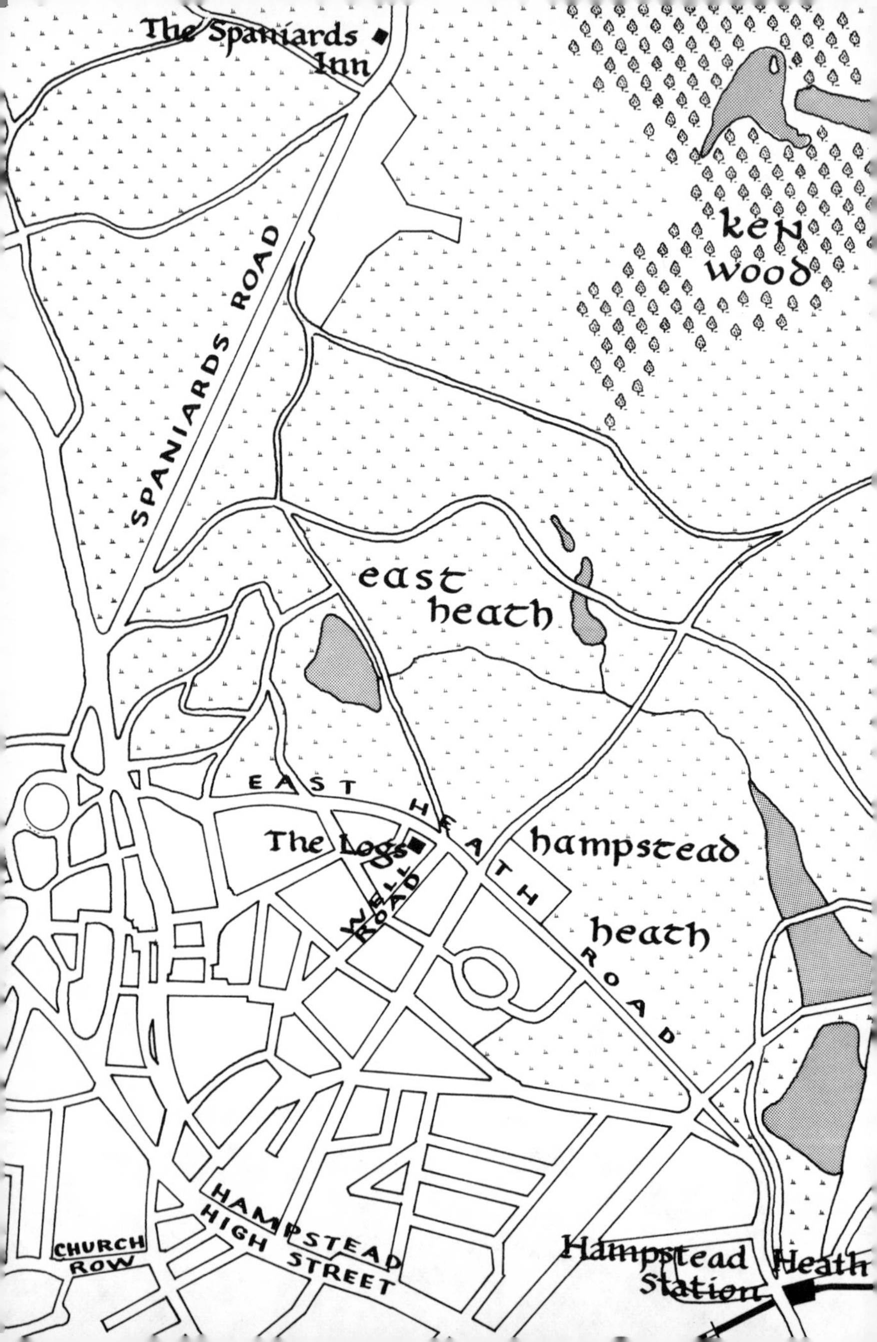
The Spaniards Inn
Ken Wood
SPANIARDS ROAD
east heath
EAST HEATH ROAD
The Logs
WELL ROAD
hampstead heath
HAMPSTEAD HIGH STREET
CHURCH ROW
Hampstead Heath Station

called "the worst man in London" was on an appropriately chilly Sunday afternoon in November. There seemed to be little profit in retracing the route of that pair of gentlemanly burglars, as the area had changed so much in eighty years, so we took the Tube, which trades scenery for speed.

We walked along East Heath Road, by the edge of the Heath, feeling vaguely cheated that we were looking for an already identified site but concerned that such a structure had not survived our egalitarian times. A walk of a few blocks brought us to Well Road, and there, at the corner, was the massive and meandering Victorian pile of The Logs. It had survived after all, and when we stole upon the grounds we learned why.

The entire scene was much as Holmes and Watson found it that tempestuous, cold January evening in 1899. It is an excellent example of the exuberance of Victorian taste, replete with a mansard tower, gables, and odd corners, done in that creamy type of brick favored in the 1870s. It is fake Gothic, but rather than creating the feeling of soaring height which is the mark of true Gothic, The Logs sits heavily upon the ground. There is a sense of brooding melancholy about the place. It frowns rather than smiles.

The wall that Watson mentioned is still there, some six feet in height, surrounding the grounds, which are a long and narrow half-block. The grounds contain many trees, including large yews, that English favorite.

The Logs has survived because it has been cut up into extensive flats, a sad fate, but not as sad as demolition, all testimony to increased population and decreased wealth. Before it was known as The Logs, it was The Lion, as the entrance at the wall attests in stone. It overlooks the southern portion of the Heath and is situated in an area still residential.

Appledore Towers as it appears today

All in all, it is the kind of residence which would have afforded to Charles Augustus Milverton those qualities of stolidity, solidity, exaggerated comfort, and a sense of permanence which the times demanded.

Michael Harrison suggests that as the Appledore burglars would logically have exited the Heath in the vicinity of the Spaniards Inn, they would have been foolish not to have availed themselves of a drink at this still excellent pub. This is a civilized suggestion, and it is pleasant to think of them safely cosseted within its comfortable walls, ceremoniously celebrating their coup with the inevitable brandy and soda, it being well after dinner. The Spaniards is a popular and ancient public house; it is sufficiently old that no one can recall the reason for its name, with divergent theories being urged, somewhat more strongly in the evening, from pirates to highwaymen to ambassadors. Outside, like many English buildings, it is nondescript, a white-painted brick building, modest in size and without any memorable architectural attribute. Inside, it is most comfortable, with ancient wooden floors indented by the thirsty traffic of centuries, a tangle of small rooms with low-beamed ceilings and companionable fires in small fireplaces.

For light refreshment, unless you are an ale aficionado, it is usually wiser to try the superb English cider, which is hard cider by American standards, or, if you are made of stronger stuff, English gin. It was gin which kept the lower classes from revolting against the State for two hundred years and kept much of the upper classes in a state which could only be classed as revolting. Unless you have been in the United Kingdom, you haven't really had English gin: it is more

The wall over which Holmes and Watson scrambled to safety following the shooting of Charles Augustus Milverton

The Spaniards Inn

delicately flavored, and it is only 70% alcohol by volume, as opposed to the 90% for export.

The Spaniards furnishes the usual pub fare: bangers, Scotch eggs, and various cold meat pies, but it also has sandwiches—after all, an English invention—with Scotch salmon between, or, for the more genteel appetite, watercress or cucumber. They are all surprisingly good here, as they are, in fact, all over England.

Hampstead is only a few minutes by Underground from central London, and you should do what many Londoners do—take a Sunday excursion to Hampstead Heath. You will understand much about the English, but, more than that, you will see an area much as it was in Holmes's day.

VII. Kingston-upon-Thames and the Baron

HOLMES AND WATSON shared one wholly hedonistic pleasure, and, except for tobacco in most forms and drug dependence, it was one of Holmes's few concessions to matters of the flesh. Turkish baths, Watson observed in *The Illustrious Client,* made Holmes more malleable than any other activity, which does not say a great deal for the detective's sensuality.

It was in a quiet corner of the second floor of Neville's establishment on Wednesday, September 3, 1902, that Holmes shared with Watson a note from a Carlton Club member which placed Holmes on a collision course with one of the most satisfyingly despicable miscreants in the entire Canon—Baron Adelbert Gruner, the arrogant Austrian with the antennae-like mustaches. Holmes's undisclosed but august client is regarded by critical scholarship as King Edward VII, who had on more than one occasion involved himself in the problems of his friends, usually to his public discomfiture. It is not surprising that he required anonymity in the de Merville matter.

The Baron resided elegantly at Vernon Lodge, an estate near Kingston, where he collected books and paintings and had become a published authority in Chinese porcelain. Watson described the dwelling, which he entered in the guise of Dr. Hill Barton, a fellow collector.

> The beautiful house and grounds indicated that Baron Gruner was . . . a man of considerable wealth. A long winding drive, with banks of rare shrubs on either side, opened out into a great gravelled square adorned with statues. The place had been built by a South African gold king in the days of the great boom, and the long, low house with the turrets at the corners, an architectural nightmare, was imposing in its size and solidity.

For the site voyeur, *The Illustrious Client* is particularly appealing. It affords a slice of aristocratic Victorian life—the Carlton Club, the Café Royal, and Kingston-upon-Thames. The obvious first choice was the Gruner mansion, as the others are well-known establishments and not subject to dispute as to their locations.

What were to become the suburbs of London had not yet merged into one continuous municipal web in 1902, and between them were still very satisfactory rural areas, which is why Holmes was advised that Gruner's residence was *near* Kingston. The allusion is to Kingston-upon-Thames, which is southwest of London, near Wimbledon and Surbiton.

On a fine, fresh spring morning, we took the train from Victoria Station—second class, my pet economy—arriving in Kingston well within the hour. Because of the large number of site possibilities, it seemed wise to enlist help, so at the cab stand at the station I made the usual tourist inquiry if any driver spoke English. It turned out that none did, although we finally located a cabby who appreciated the challenge we posed, and he was even able to suggest some additional locations. I would have mentioned him by name, but he opted for cash.

Kingston has retained its role as a beautiful and expensive suburb. There are many splendid homes here, some of the vintage of Baron Gruner's day but many of more recent

Kingston-upon-Thames was the scene of the coronation of the Saxon kings a thousand years ago. For centuries afterward, London Bridge and the bridge at Kingston were the only permanent structures spanning the Thames. In keeping with its historic importance – and its regal traditions – Kingston in the late nineteenth century found favor with the *nouveaux riches* who built their often palatial homes here within easy commuting distance of London.

construction. Except for those fortunate homes which have been institutionalized into schools or business headquarters, the old mansions have succumbed to what are euphemistically termed land developers, who, with the magic of modern commercial alchemy, have transformed the area into egalitarian drab.

The search for the Baron's palatial retreat appeared to be doomed from the start. It was not possible to tell in which direction from the town center the Lodge was situated, or even how far. We are vouchsafed few specifics. Nor did the name Vernon Lodge connote anything which could be related to another mansion. Vernon was an English admiral who has a fine wine named after him.

Our first stop on that May-bright day was The Pavillion, a brilliant white two-story dwelling with extremely long windows, all done in the style of a restrained Trianon transplanted to the South of France. It is tasteful and wholly alien to Victorian style-borrowings. Even the driver felt its un-English overtones, and we hurried on to see nearby Warren House. It is false Tudor, large and rambling, and could function unobtrusively on any American campus. More significantly for our purpose, it does not meet the characteristics which Watson furnished. With a sense of beginning dis-ease, we traveled to Coombe Hill, the next nearest possibility. The long uphill entrance drive, bordered by ancient elms, raised our hopes, which quickly receded again as our cab made a right-hand turn and we saw the authentic Tudor pile which would have been built at least three hundred years before Baron Gruner graced this island. Coombe Hill, now the corporate headquarters of a television company, does have obviously late additions, but, had this been the Baron's lair, Watson's description would have been much different. It just does not fit.

Our cabbie could sense our disappointment and suggested as a likely candidate a house he described as large and old. Four Acres was its designation, an authentic Elizabethan home with a timbered-and-plaster exterior, and from it I learned two things: first that "old" in England means three hundred years or more, and second that this also was not the house. Having noticed that the clubhouses of English golf clubs are often former manor houses or almost-stately homes, I asked the cabbie to take us to the local golf club, which turned out to have what was apparently the only new clubhouse in Britain.

At Coombe Hill, I had been advised that one of the writers for the local newspaper was interested in the large homes of the area and that she might have written about some of them. We repaired to the newspaper office, as there were one or two homes which had been destroyed in the last few years past. We were unable to locate the newspaperwoman, and her articles did not furnish any information about any house which could have been the original of Vernon Lodge.

The newspaper office was on the square, and the local marketeers were out with barrows and stalls. The square was filled with flowers for sale, and it was easy to visualize what a medieval fair here would have been like. After a late, light, but restorative lunch, some dismay had gone, and we were ready to go back to London.

It had begun to rain, one of those sudden, squall-like English rains which last for a few minutes and are gone. Before going to the station, we directed the cab driver, for no real reason, to swing by the area we had visited in the morning. Through the light rain, I could see a large residence which seemed, at least fleetingly, to meet some of Watson's description. The taxi screeched to a stop two hundred or so feet away, and, while it backed up, I hurried to the house. There was indeed a winding drive and a square, but the corners were not turreted nor was the residence low. No statuary was present, but that is not a significant omission.

The house, red brick, is long but not low, being both two and three stories, with a pseudo-Romanesque tower and some

ersatz Elizabethan touches, and otherwise constitutes an undistinguished copy of late Victorian Gothic.

Architectonic mass can be deceptive, and a tall house may appear to be low because of its length, such as here. Moreover, long and low houses were neither the taste nor style of the period, when pseudo-Gothic influences dictated height and volume, and it is submitted that Watson was either indiscriminate in his observations or vague in his recollections.

If the spirit of the thing is significant, this mansion, now Holy Cross Preparatory School, could well have been the evil Baron's English abode. It possesses the heavy pretentiousness of the period and is the very house which would have appealed to the baroque sense of an Austrian nobleman, but, while clearly meeting Watson's test of an architectural nightmare, it is not the structure as described by him. At best it remains a provisional attribution for Vernon Lodge which should suffice until a long, low mansion with turrets on the corners is unearthed near Kingston-upon-Thames.

◄ Vernon Lodge today – still "an architectural nightmare. . . imposing in its size and solidity."

VIII.
Down the Old Kent Road

HAD Holmes varied his pleasures from the violin blandishments of Sarasate and Norman-Neruda, or descended from the Albert and St. James's Halls to one of the many London music halls, he would have been familiar with that popular ballad "Wot Cher (Knocked 'Em in the Old Kent Road)." And, possessed of that knowledge, he might have mused upon it while driving down the same road that June night in 1889 *en route* to Neville St. Clair's villa, The Cedars, on the outskirts of Lee.

Lee at the time of *The Man with the Twisted Lip* was an upper-middle-class village in the southeastern suburbs. A few miles beyond is Chislehurst, which in the early 1870s had been Napoleon III's place of exile. He had leased Camden Place, which has survived into our day as a private golf club and which has been advanced as one of the many possibilities for the Abbey Grange. Lee itself was the home of John Scott Eccles, who would figure prominently in the Wisteria Lodge tragedy a few years hence. Scott Eccles resided at Popham House—still unidentified—and represented the establishment Englishman of his time. Careful of place, he would not have lived in a quarter which did not provide a backdrop of sterling respectability.

My winter scrutiny of fairly detailed maps of the area disclosed no estate named The Cedars, but east of Lee, between the Eltham Road (which is the continuation of the

Lee High Road) and Westhorne Avenue, was a winding street called Cedarhurst Drive. It is not uncommon in England to perpetuate in the new streets the name of an estate which has been subdivided. Cedarhurst drive could be a permutation of The Cedars. "Hurst" means a rise or a wooded eminence and is of geographical rather than historical significance.*

Cedarhurst Drive was my only possibility, and accordingly, one wet spring morning, Audrey and I drove out the few miles from central London. Like Holmes and Watson, we took A2, which is the Old Kent Road, then A20, which is Lewisham Way and the Lee High Road.

We did encounter some difficulty in communicating with the local populace. The English use their language with a precision that Americans find unnecessary, and they are very helpful, so you can count on very explicit directions. I will never forget: "Go straight down this street, deny yourself two turnings, and it's the next house but one." British directions have been compared to a lawyer's advice—lengthy and correct, but not helpful.

On our way this day, we spent many precious minutes trying to find I-205, that being the motorway a friendly native in a nearby store had recommended to Audrey. After repeated failures, I asked her in my most pleasant loud voice to repeat the *exact* instructions. She repeated: "You toike I-205," and it was apparent even to one not indigenous that the A205 sign which we had been seeing was the proper road.

---

*My maps also disclosed a Boone Street and a Boone's Road in Lee, which added some eerie confirmation to my search and raised the question as to whether this was the source of Hugh Boone's last name.

And while we did find A205 and Cedarhurst Drive, we failed to find The Cedars. Cedarhurst Drive was part of a subdivision—our hunch was correct in that respect—but it is a series of similarly-built and similarly-situated tract houses. They are the proud products of the egalitarian twentieth century—uniform, unoriginal, and without any saving eccentricity. It was not an area where a Neville St. Clair would live, but unfortunately it is probably suitable for his great-grandchildren.

The conclusion was fairly evident. The Cedars had not survived the years since 1889, or, if it had, we had exhausted both our time and our leads. Disappointed, we pressed on to Chislehurst in search of the Abbey Grange, where the problem was a surplus of possible sites rather than their absence, and not a satisfactory choice to be made among them.

Thus the matter of The Cedars stood for several years, until Kentish resident Kelvin I. Jones reported in his book *Sherlock Holmes and the South-Eastern* that it had survived, outwardly intact but by the 1920s divided into flats, and that it was located on Belmont Hill. This was heady information and sufficiently definite to make further inquiry worthwhile. So it was on a sunny Bank Holiday Monday (Whitsuntide for the religious) that I traveled by train from Victoria Station to Lewisham, a matter of only a few minutes. I had inadvertently selected one of the English high holidays when Britons worship at the seashore and everything closes down. Lewisham was devoid of cabs, and there was no answer when I dialed the taxi company. I was becoming restive, and I complained of the moribund transportation network of Lewisham to two pleasant police constables parked in their nearby cruiser. The mention of Sherlock Holmes opens even the doors of police cars, and P.C.s Smith and Edwards offered to assist in my quest for "a large villa which stood within its own grounds." On our way to Belmont Hill, which is a street extending at a right angle eastward from Lewisham Way, they radioed an inquiry to the station, but no one had heard of The Cedars.

We drove the entire length of Belmont Hill, unsuccessfully searching for likely candidates, and indeed had gone way past St. Margaret's parish church, Belmont Hill having become Lee Terrace, when it was apparent that we had missed the villa, if it still really existed. Retracing our route, one of the constables remarked in an offhand manner that there was a convent and school behind the wall which we were passing. "Drive back," I urged, knowing from my experience that this was the sort of place which afforded a likelihood of success.

We drove down the "small, winding gravel drive," although it was paved now, a minor and not disabling element. Huge bushes crowded against the drive, and around the first short turn there was a glimpse of the corner of a large, dazzling white stone mansion house, replete with corner quoins. We stopped before an imposing white entrance. There were Regency overtones and an elegant roof balustrade. One of the constables went to the door and flushed a rather excited nun, from whom he inquired if this were called The Cedars. She replied that it was not, but that it once had been.

I spent a delightful half-day at the Convent of the Sacred Hearts of Jesus and Mary in the courteous hands of Sister Rita, the headmistress, and Sister Monica, as well as coveys of other sisters who floated in and out of the sitting room. The students of Sister Rita had recently written a history of the house for the student newspaper, and she obligingly furnished me with a copy. According to the article, the mansion had been built around 1738 and was originally named Lee

The Cedars, Lee

Grove. The cedars from which it later took its name were planted by a Miss Boyfield, who was the owner from 1810 to 1820. The property was later sold to Samuel Brandram and passed to his nephew, John Thomas Brandram, after whose death in 1855 it was sold to John Penn. It was Penn who changed the name of the estate from Lee Grove to The Cedars. The sisters also provided me with *The Story of Lee,* written in 1923 by Messrs. R. R. C. Gregory and F. W. Nunn, which disclosed that Penn had been a manufacturer of marine engines and during the Crimean War became something of a national hero. By using assembly-line methods, he built a prodigious number of gunboats in a short space of time. His oscillating engines were used on the British Royal yacht *Victoria and Albert,* on Franz Josef's *Miramar,* and on the Turkish Sultan's yacht. Penn died in 1878, and, again according to the student publication, his widow continued to reside at The Cedars until the First World War.

Watson's account differs somewhat in that, according to Holmes, who was a stickler for accuracy, Neville St. Clair acquired the estate in 1884.

The history reasonably in mind, I was accorded a tour of the public portions of the structure. The house was a large one, with spacious rooms comfortably situated. The sisters' furniture neither sought nor achieved the elegance of the house, but the walls and ceilings still showed beautiful appointments. I did not press to see the two rooms occupied by Holmes when he stayed here in 1889 and where his cerebration, five pillows, and an ounce of shag had solved the mystery of Hugh Boone and restored a repentant Neville St. Clair to his wife and children.

Before I left, Sister Monica conducted me around the reduced grounds, which still afford a rare and vital view of Victorian England when it had dominion over palm and pine. Here is an authenticated site, and I hoped that St. Clair, newly restored to his friends and relations, enjoyed a long and pleasant life here, untroubled by the reappearance of *The Man with the Twisted Lip.*

At right: "Oxshott Common" has altered not at all since Sherlock Holmes walked here during the Wisteria Lodge case

The
Home Counties

IX.
Investigations in Surrey

HOLMES himself undertook several forays into Surrey, now as then one of London's bedroom counties, first in 1883 to Stoke Moran to assist the distraught Miss Helen Stoner and later in 1895 to rescue Miss Violet Smith, who was nearly equally imperiled, and in between he was able to resolve the perplexities of John Scott Eccles and bring the Reigate squires to heel.

The exploration of these four sites could conveniently be done at the same time, as they are no more than a few miles apart.* Esher, where Holmes and Watson investigated the adventure of *Wisteria Lodge,* is only a few minutes southwest of London, and it was here that we too began the investigation into the location of Wisteria Lodge itself.

We knew from the Canon that even the respectable and utterly placid John Scott Eccles had second thoughts about having accepted the sudden invitation of his newly-met acquaintance, Aloysius Garcia, when he saw that Wisteria Lodge was "an old, tumble-down building in a crazy state of

---

*A fifth, Briarbrae, the Harrison home in *The Naval Treaty,* was located "among the fir woods and the heather of Woking," also in Surrey, and is of more than passing interest because of the vital national considerations involved in the case. The identification of Briarbrae is disputed, but the two attributions, Inchcape House and Woodham Hall, are both destroyed.

disrepair." If it were not for the promise of the culinary triumphs of the wonderful half-breed cook about whom Garcia had boasted, he probably would have turned in his tracks.

Wisteria Lodge, according to Scott Eccles, was about two miles south of Esher, fair-sized, and "standing back from the road, with a curving drive which was banked with high evergreen shrubs."

According to Watson, it was near the end of March 1892,† around 6:00 P.M., when Holmes and Watson arrived at Esher, accompanied by Inspector Baynes of the Surrey constabulary. Together they walked about two miles to Wisteria Lodge through the cold, driving March rain. "A cold and melancholy walk of a couple of miles brought us to a high wooden gate, which opened into a gloomy avenue of chestnuts. The curved and shadowed drive led us to a low, dark house, pitch-black against a slate-coloured sky."

Watson notes that the road from Esher took them through the "wild common." The road is still there: Copsem Lane, extending some four miles between Esher and Oxshott and traversing Esher Common. The area remains heavily wooded, with a few homes clinging here and there to the road.

A "common" is another one of those terms connoting different things on each side of the Atlantic. In America it is a well-manicured greensward in the middle of a town, usually in New England, while in England it refers to undivided and

---

† A year universally disputed by Holmesian savants, as in 1892 Holmes was engaged upon his mysterious Tibetan travels.

HERSHAM
ESHER
River Mole
PORTSMOUTH ROAD
COPSEM LANE
CLAYGATE
esher common
STOKESHEATH ROAD
QUEEN'S DRIVE
Queen Anne House
oxshott heath
OXSHOTT
COBHAM
STOKE ROAD
River
STOKE D'ABERNON
Plough Inn
woodlands park
Manor House
Mole
Slyfield House
LEATHERHEAD

unenclosed land, or even wasteland, which is open to public use.

Watson does not materially assist in the identification of Wisteria Lodge, hardly a surprising revelation, when he observes that the patriot Garcia, who had leased the Lodge, was found dead "upon Oxshott Common, nearly a mile from his home." While the distance could be of some assistance, Watson has otherwise confused Oxshott Heath with the adjacent Esher Common.

If Watson's description of the Esher-to-Wisteria Lodge walk that raw March evening is substantially accurate, the Lodge is not too far distant from the Heath Road. The villa has historically been placed in the region between Esher Common and Oxshott Heath, slightly to the southwest of Esher and west of the old road between Esher and Leatherhead. Despite a careful scrutiny and a retracing of the route more than once, we found no dwellings along the road which had either the antiquity or the style of the original Wisteria Lodge. As was our practice, we then proceeded to extend the search farther out from the area originally proposed. Eastward from Copsem Lane, and somewhat less than four miles south of Esher, is a Crown Estate, which has been subdivided with the usual results. Antedating the subdivision, and surrounded by woods, is a large red-brick home. It is situated in Queen's Drive near Stokesheath Road, which would have been the entrance before the development. It is called Queen Anne House.

This dwelling possesses the remains of the requisite curved driveway. Watson described Wisteria Lodge as a low house, and, while Queen Anne House is not low, it does have that appearance because of its steep roof and the small windows on the first (American second) floor.

Wisteria Lodge

If it is Wisteria Lodge—and the identification is not definitive—some householder subsequent to the late Aloysius Garcia has been kind to the estate and has restored it from disrepair and disarray.

There is a further attribution to be considered, and that is "the famous old Jacobean grange of High Gable, one mile on the farther side of Oxshott, and less than half a mile from the scene of the tragedy." This was the refuge of Don Juan Murillo, the bushy-browed Tiger of San Pedro.

We are given the clues of the house's Jacobean architecture, its fame, and its approximate location. A grange connotes a gentleman farmer's establishment, and we can infer that its particular architectural feature is its single high gable. It awaits precise location, but is a likely candidate for early identification.

There is a final attribution which can be made with considerable assurance. Holmes and Watson stayed for several days at Esher in connection with the Wisteria Lodge matter and "found comfortable quarters at the Bull." There is no Bull, but there is a Bear Inn in Esher, which still stands on the main village street where it is intersected by the road to

The inn at which Holmes and Watson stayed during the Wisteria Lodge investigation

Oxshott. It would have been a hostelry convenient to Wisteria Lodge.

It is curious why Watson failed to accurately identify the inn. He plainly identified Brambletye in the case of *Black Peter,* and there was nothing which would have caused any embarrassment to the proprietor of the Bear by the inclusion of his establishment in the story. The most likely explanation is that the good doctor forgot the correct name.

* * *

Watson portrayed the case of *The Speckled Band* as possessing more unusual facets than any other in which he and Holmes were involved. It is probably the all-time favorite of non-Sherlockians and near the top of the list for dedicated followers of the Canon. The adventure began, as did the most satisfying of all of them, at Baker Street, with an interview with a distraught young woman, in this case a Miss Helen Stoner, of the Manor House of Stoke Moran.

When on April 6, 1883, Holmes and Watson arrived at Stoke Moran, near Leatherhead, in Surrey, they saw the mouldering mansion of the Roylotts, situated in a grove at the top of a "heavily timbered. . .gentle slope." The house was described by Watson as being of "gray, lichen-blotched stone, with a high central portion and two curving wings, like the claws of a crab, thrown out on each side. In one of these wings the windows were broken and blocked with wooden boards, while the roof was partly caved in, a picture of ruin."

Watson and Holmes stayed at the Crown Inn, which commanded a view of the avenue gate and the inhabited wing of the Manor House.

Michael Harrison identified Stoke Moran as being Stoke d'Abernon, placing the Manor House somewhere between

Slyfield House and Woodlands Park. Harrison believed the house itself to have been razed, and there is some canonical authority for this supposition. The house was, in Miss Stoner's words, "crushed under a heavy mortgage," and her income was minimal. The site of two fearful deaths cannot have been an inducement to her to remain. Undoubtedly, she married her Percy Armitage, of Crane Water, near Reading, and they lived far away from Stoke Moran, the scene of what Watson described as a "most dark and sinister business."

Two crucial questions remain: Where was the Roylott mansion, and did it survive?

Harrison's analysis of the location, and his identification of Stoke Moran with Stoke d'Abernon, are sufficiently persuasive as to be conclusive, and there is a similarity of names which fits Watsonian geographical ingenuity and genteel duplicity.

Stoke d'Abernon is still a delightful Surrey village, not yet overwhelmed by London suburbia, although no more than an hour away by car. There are some housing projects in the town, and south of the village the roads are, as the British claim, metalled, but otherwise things were much the same in April 1979 as in April 1883.

Local tradition clearly identifies the Roylott estate with Woodlands Park, which possesses one of the notable gardens of England. It was an obvious first stop, and the residence does carry an ominous ambience of impending doom. It is a sprawling, red-brick structure, with a central fake-Gothic tower in the style of late Victorian times. Architecturally, it is probably too recent for the Roylott establishment. There is, however, a more obvious drawback—there is no nearby inn. The Canon is most explicit that, from their quarters at the inn, Watson and Holmes could see the avenue gate and the inhabited wing of the Manor House. This was of vital and overwhelming significance, as Miss Stoner was to signal to them in the inn when all was quiet at the Manor. She did, at 11:00 P.M., and the grotesque culmination of this singular adventure followed.

The inn is still there, furnishing cheer to the grandchildren of its 1883 patrons. It is not the Crown Inn mentioned by Watson, and never was, but Watson's custom of literary obfuscation is generally recognized. Its clientele for many generations have known it as the Plough Inn, and it is not much changed from Holmes's time.

Now that we had found the inn, we could look for a manor house within an easy view. The barmaid, while serving up some fine hard cider, cheerfully obliged with some helpful information. There was a big house thereabouts, south on

The Crown Inn as Holmes knew it during the case of the Speckled Band

Stoke Road, which ran along the east side of the Plough. There was a straight view south from the inn, and any one of the three upstairs windows would afford an easy view the half-mile or so to the house, though some new housing flats now effectively blocked the prospect which existed in the 1880s. She also served one additional bit of information—the view was of the Manor House. My wife and I looked at each other meaningfully over the cider.

Hurriedly driving down Stoke Road, we saw the iron gate as described by Watson, and, entering the access road, we noted with satisfaction that the Manor House was at the top of a slight, well-timbered slope, also as Watson had described. The Manor was not Watson's lichen-blotched stone in mouldering decay, nor were there gray stones, but elegant, rambling red brick in the Queen Anne style. The survival of

The Crown has changed virtually not at all during the last century.

Stoke Moran

the mansion has been assured by an institutional tenant, the I.L.E.A., an organization of teachers.

It is arguable that the Roylott Manor House was never constructed of stone, and that this was another Watsonian substitution—the same as the Crown Inn for the Plough—to afford Miss Stoner the anonymity she required. Remember that Watson prefaced his story with the fact that he could at last publish his recollections because a promise of secrecy had been ended by Miss Stoner's death, which indicates that he wrote the adventure from his notes prior to her passing. This could well account for a deliberate variance of the architectural hallmarks.

Or it may be that, as great houses were added to at different times and with differing styles in a form of architectural accretion, the stone portion was later leveled, and, if the mansion were in the decaying state chronicled by Watson, this is not surprising.

The same peaceful English countryside which masked Dr.

Grimesby Roylott's crimes at the Manor House remains much the same today, awaiting those semi-adventurous spirits who wish to convert Holmes and Watson's journey to Stoke Moran into a pilgrimage.

* * *

It is difficult in our time of accelerated and overwhelming technological and moral change to understand the concern and indignation associated with the advent of the bicycle. Miss Violet Smith, one of these daring cyclists, is one of the Canon's heroines, and her story is recounted in the adventure of *The Solitary Cyclist.* It was the queenly Miss Smith who pedaled her bicycle, doubtlessly at an acceptably ladylike pace, from Chiltern Grange past Charlington Heath and Charlington Hall to Farnham and into the Holmes saga.

Having been reduced in circumstances by her father's death, Miss Smith had accepted a position at Chiltern Grange, "about six miles from Farnham," as a music teacher for the daughter of Bob Carruthers, who had known Miss Smith's uncle in South Africa. Farnham is in Surrey in the midst of the North Downs.

It was on her Saturday bicycling trips from Chiltern Grange to Farnham Station, to entrain for her usual London weekend with her mother, that she found herself followed by an unidentified bearded man who, in proper Victorian fashion, "kept his distance and did not molest" her. It was the presence of this disconcerting follower which caused Miss Smith to call upon Sherlock Holmes.

With the six-mile reference point, it had been possible to exclude certain areas. Michael Harrison, in his *In the Footsteps of Sherlock Holmes,* eliminates the road to Aldershot, as Aldershot itself is only three miles from Farnham. As

Haslemere, another railway station, is approximately ten miles from Farnham, Chiltern Grange cannot be along the Haslemere Road, for, if it were, Miss Smith would have ridden the four miles to Haslemere rather than the six miles to Farnham. Likewise, the road to Alton can be excluded because the distance between Alton and Farnham is also ten miles. The Guildford Road, too, is not a possibility because the distance from Farnham is approximately ten miles. There are roads to the west of Farnham, and one of them could have been the route of the Solitary Cyclist; this is unlikely, however, because when Miss Smith described where in the country she was living, she said, "near Farnham, on the borders of Surrey." The Surrey border with Hampshire is no more than two miles west of Farnham. Since Chiltern Grange was six miles from Farnham, if it were west it would have been at least four miles into Hampshire. Had the Grange been so situated, surely Miss Smith would not have given a location with reference to Surrey, but rather would have said near Farnham, but in Hampshire.

This leaves the road to Milford, which runs generally southeastward, a conclusion reached by Harrison early on.

The canonical geographical descriptions of that part of Surrey on those April Saturdays of 1895 are surprisingly explicit, perhaps because the malefactors were criminal and Miss Smith could in no way be embarrassed by a disclosure of the facts. She described her route to Farnham with admirable specificity:

"The road from Chiltern Grange is a lonely one, and at one spot it is particularly so, for it lies for over a mile between Charlington Heath upon one side and the woods which lie round Charlington Hall upon the other. You could not find a more lonely tract of road anywhere, and it is quite rare to meet so much as a cart, or a peasant, until you reach the high road near Crooksbury Hill."

Harrison has concluded that Crooksbury Hill is Monk's Hill, which he opines is a more likely identification than Crooksbury Heath, all being in the Charleshill area, which is on the north side of the road from Farnham to Milford.

Charlington Hall, or at least its chimney and roof, was visible from the hill. This Hall, the residence of those villains Woodley and Williamson, boasted a "main gateway of lichen-studded stone, each side pillar surmounted by mouldering heraldic emblems," with the house not being visible from the road, despite the gaps in the old yew hedge. Watson

The road down which Violet Smith was pursued by the "solitary cyclist" on her way to Farnham Station

described the grounds as manifesting "gloom and decay," and the house, as he peered through the trees, was described as an "old gray building with. . . bristling Tudor chimneys." Chiltern Grange is innocent of description, as the dramatic action all occurred on the grounds of Charlington Hall.

While Michael Harrison was unable to identity either Charlington Hall or Chiltern Grange, he did find some homes in the Charleshill vicinity which fit the canonical descriptions, except that none was located within its own substantial grounds. This is not surprising in view of the many social, geographic, and demographic changes which occurred between the time of the adventure in 1895 and the appearance of his book in 1960. Those manorial establishments which have survived tract developments, loss of servants and the evaporation of the comfortable wealth of an empire have been long since shorn of their baronial park-like settings.

With these data at hand, we were prepared to start from the Farnham end and, by following the Milford road eastward, to come upon Charlington Hall. The route between Farnham and Milford is no longer the "broad sandy road" of 1895. It is paved, but it remains otherwise substantially the same—an area of tangled woods and steep hills with narrow and contented valleys. The road sinks deeply into the hills, with tangled branches extending protectively over portions of the road. Houses are few and sit well within their own grounds. Wood smoke from more than one fireplace added a pleasant dimension to the search.

There is in the western part of Charleshill, a very small and rural community, a gray mansion by the River Wey, north of the road, replete with bristling chimneys. The property has many trees and still possesses ample space for the

Charlington Hall

fake wedding and its surprising dénouement. If this is not Charlington Hall, it could well be, and it seems somehow appropriate, although some owner since 1895 has restored it lovingly. If it is Charlington Hall, then Chiltern Grange would be east of Charleshill by no more than two miles, and west of Elstead.

If there is a lack of resolution as to the location of Charlington Hall and Chiltern Grange, there is no question as to the identity of the Farnham railway station, where Miss Smith left her bicycle and departed for London. It remains

Farnham Station today, little changed from the 1890s

still, and without any apparent exterior changes from those Saturdays in 1895 when she would take the 12:22 to the Metropolis.

There still remain in Surrey pleasant country towns like Stoke d'Abernon and Charleshill, with some vestiges of dwellings of a pleasanter time, once inhabited by those who never in their wildest imaginings conceived of a tax on either income or capital.

* * *

The Surrey town of Reigate, on the main road between Gatwick Airport and London, is only about eight miles from Oxshott and Stoke d'Abernon. It is the site of a significant Holmes adventure—*The Reigate Squires,* renamed *The*

Reigate Puzzle in U.S. editions, apparently out of anticipated concern for American suspicions of British aristocracy. The mystery was solved because of Holmes's fortuitous presence at Colonel Hayter's bachelor establishment near Reigate during that spring of 1887. Watson had treated Colonel Hayter in Afghanistan, and the colonel had invited both Watson and Holmes to the house which he had leased near Reigate. Holmes required recuperation from his overwork in unmasking the immense financial schemes of Baron Maupertuis and the Netherland-Sumatra Company, and so it was to the Hayter digs near Reigate to which they repaired. Colonel Hayter's house has not been identified and probably will never be identifiable, as there are insufficient data, and we have the Master's own warning about such theorizing. Holmes's instincts picked up on the rather odd little robbery at old Acton's, but he was persuaded by Watson to forego any further inquiry into the matter until word arrived at breakfast that, during an attempted night burglary at Justice of the Peace Cunningham's, William the coachman had been shot through the heart.

Cunningham and his son lived in a "fine red Queen Anne house, which bears the date of Malplaquet upon the lintel of the door." There was a lodge house, a "pretty cottage" where the victim, William Kirwin, had lived with his aged mother. Beyond the lodge house and extending to the Cunningham home was an oak-lined avenue.

Two houses have been proposed as that fine old Queen Anne house. These are Gatton Hall, near Reigate, and the Priory, which is within Reigate proper. I had written from America to the mayor of the borough of Reigate and Banstead, and he had obligingly furnished not only a 96-page *Official Guide to the Borough of Reigate and Banstead* but specific information about both prospects. He advised that Gatton Hall was for some fifty years the seat of Sir Jeremiah Colman but was destroyed by fire in 1936 and rebuilt thereafter on smaller dimensions. A colonnade is all that remains from the original structure. The estate is presently the Royal Alexandra and Abbey School and is under the patronage of H.M. Queen Elizabeth.

The Priory still stands, now officially termed the Reigate Priory Middle School, and is situated by Bell Street in Reigate.

We were spending the night at Chiddingfold, a small village near Haslemere and some sixteen miles southwest of Reigate. The attraction was the Crown, a comfortable coaching inn with fifteenth-century antecedents, whose worn and uneven peg floors testified to a long patronage. We had tried several times over fifteen years to stay there, but one thing or another had interfered. The late April weather was cold and the space heater in the room welcome. I spread the Reigate papers on the comforter of the ancient fourposter, its ebony-black wood worn smooth by the hands of tired travelers through the centuries. A sharp wind outside rattled the small-paned windows. Audrey claimed it reminded her of the Admiral Benbow Inn in *Treasure Island* the night it was attacked.

We had only one prospect in Reigate, and our hopes were accordingly not high. The next morning, after an early breakfast in our room of tea, marmalade, and English muffins, we drove to Reigate. With the assistance of the *Official Guide,* we found the Priory quickly. It was located within a large park, Reigate Park, and there was a long, tree-lined approach, although I did not note if they were oaks as Watson stated. The Priory was indeed in the style of Queen Anne, and a fine specimen it was. Two stories in height, in

The fine old Queen Anne house where dwelt the Reigate squires still stands, its elegance undiminished.

the form of a modified H in front, it was both large and tasteful, always a difficult accomplishment. While meeting the essential fine Queen Anne requirement, it was not red but gray with corner quoins. There was a small central clock tower and, beneath it, on the triangular pediment, a coat of arms. Regrettably, the date of the Battle of Malplaquet, 1706, or any date, is missing, but the allusion may only have been Watsonian literary license. The interiors have been changed since the last private owner transferred it to the public in 1922. The exterior remains the same, however, and is graceful and elegant. Holmes, Watson, Colonel Hayter, Inspector Forrester of the Surrey force, and the two Cunninghams inspected the first floor at Holmes's instance. Several bedrooms and the drawing room were here, which would be the second floor in American parlance. That they faced the front of the house, which would be the south, we know from Holmes's observation. The murderous attack upon Holmes occurred within the dressing room of the younger Cunningham, which would be one of the eleven windows on the second floor south.

The house neatly corresponds to Dr. Watson's description of the "fine old Queen Anne house" which was the seat of the murderous Cunninghams. It is significant as the site of one of Holmes's few miscalculations and the resulting dramatic conclusion.

X.
Shoscombe Old Place

It required only a few pages to obtain Holmes's solution to the macabre mystery of Shoscombe Old Place, but it would require many more to attempt to ascertain its likely locale, largely because of Watson's lean and laconic geographic references.

The British are inveterate animal lovers, from budgerigars to dogs, and one of the kingdom's recent stamp issues features notable horses. Watson cheerfully acknowledged that about half his wound pension went for racing bets, and the turf accountants are still an honored and busy breed, thanks to a national penchant for gambling.

The central figure in the adventure is Sir Robert Norberton, a post-Regency libertine. Sir Robert was one of those time-warped sports whose proclivities were not matched to the most appropriate age in which to live; late Victorian ladies, however, like their Regency counterparts, and those today, were not insensitive to the charms of aging roués and absolute rotters.

Quite predictably, Sir Robert lived with his widowed sister, Lady Beatrice Falder, who was graced with a life estate in Shoscombe Old Place in Berkshire, where she bred the famous Shoscombe spaniels and the even more celebrated racing horse, Shoscombe Prince.

Something was terribly wrong at Lady Beatrice's estate. The dogs spurned their mistress and Sir Robert was spending an inordinate number of late-night hours in the Falder family crypt. It was this latter activity which caused John Mason, Sir Robert's head trainer, to voice that memorable question which could serve for all Gothic mysteries: "What is the master doing down at the old church crypt at night?"

The Falder estate is stated to have been situated in Berkshire, some three miles from the town of Crendall. The manor house was located within the confines of a large park with high gates surmounted by "heraldic griffins towering above." The property had been in the family so many years that, as the lawyers say, the memory of man runneth not to the contrary, and the mouldering old crypt contained family members from Norman times.

At the instance of John Mason, then, Holmes and Watson found themselves, with all manner of fishing gear, train-bound for the Green Dragon in Berkshire on Tuesday, May 6, 1902.

The reader will not be surprised to learn that there is no noble Berkshire family named Falder, nor any Berkshire town of Crendall, nor even any Green Dragon Inn. Whether from a medical concern for confidentiality or from the legal concern of invasion of privacy, Watson in this case is wary with the names of people and places.

Shoscombe is not a wholly contrived name. My winter evenings with English maps disclosed such a village in Somerset, some six miles from Bath. A Crendall could not be located, and certainly not in the county of Berkshire, which is just west of London and includes the Thames Valley. I checked all names which might transpose to Crendall and then cross-checked them against inns located there. One of the most possible of the possibilities was Cookham, a Thames-side village just north of Maidenhead. On consulting

Shoscombe Old Place

Michelin's *Great Britain,* I discovered pay dirt, for there, on Cookham High Street, was the Bel and Dragon Inn, which has a good likelihood of being Watson's Green Dragon.

Cookham is only a few miles beyond Heathrow, from which airport we were scheduled to depart, and so the morning of our departure from England found us there. It is one of those little rustic towns once rural and now suburban. It is clean and half-timbered-quaint and could be any small English village.

Because the Falder mansion is not described in the Canon, it is impossible to identify it. The meagre information given, a lake and a gate entrance, are common to many old manors, as are the family chapel and crypt, and the absence of lakes and gate entrances after 75 years is not unusual. There are three possible Shoscombes, but none is three miles from town. The first is Lullebrook Manor, which abuts the Thames, a tall and stately white edifice not attributable to any recognized style but with the strongest overtones being Regency. It is presently known as the Odney Club, a private club for the employees of one of Britain's largest department stores. Nearby Formosa Court, built by Admiral Sir George Young in 1785 and now demolished, would not have been Shoscombe Old Place because it was situated on an island, which would have been such a significant feature as to have been noted by Watson. A more likely candidate is Moor Hall, a towering and massive example of Victorian English Gothic, trading, with proper English restraint, exuberance for stolidity. There are massive gateposts, but any heraldic griffins are missing. It is now the Institute of Marketing, whose royal patron is H.R.H. Prince Philip, Duke of Edinburgh.

Holmes solved the mystery in record time, but, evidently from a natural antipathy to Sir Robert, required the reporting of the matter to the police. Shoscombe Prince nonetheless did win the Derby, and Sir Robert thereby acquired a sufficient competence to satisfy his many creditors and lay the groundwork for a creditable life, thus making this adventure one of the relatively few which was a beginning and not an end.

At right: "In the country of the Broads," where Sherlock Holmes discovered his vocation

XI.
The East Coast

MOST of Holmes's cases occurred in the counties near London, which are known as the Home Counties. There are, however, three cases clearly identified with the East of England—one in Essex and two in neighboring Norfolk. Both shires are low-lying and level, front the North Sea, and are criss-crossed with streams and dikes. They are not unlike the Netherlands, and indeed one of the English Charleses induced many Hollanders to settle here in the successful hope of draining the marshlands. Some placenames still testify to their sturdy influence.

Holmes's first and last cases occurred in the East of England. The first investigation, and the one which caused him to seriously consider becoming a consulting detective, was of course *The Gloria Scott* and arose from his acceptance of an invitation from his only university friend, young Trevor, to visit his family estate in Norfolk. Norfolk is generally regarded as the most wealthy county in England, and it is here, at Sandringham, near King's Lynn, that the Royal family has its estate, beloved of four English monarchs, and still the site of that family's Christmas celebration. This is also the county in which E. Phillips Oppenheim's finest spy story, *The Great Impersonation,* took place.

It was again to Norfolk, in his middle years, that Holmes traveled to avenge the death of his client, Hilton Cubitt, and his last case occurred in nearby Essex in August of 1914, when empires rather than persons were the stakes.

In 1912, Holmes reluctantly left his retirement eyrie on the cliffs of the South Downs, transforming himself from Holmes, the English patriot, into Altamont, the English-hating Irish-American. This, his last role, took him to Chicago, then to an Irish secret society at Buffalo, thence to Skibbereen on the smugglers' coast of Ireland, and finally into the employ of the famous German intelligence agent Von Bork. Altamont, with his goatee, could well have passed as a caricature of Uncle Sam.

As a double agent, Holmes had furnished the usual catastrophically misleading information, resulting in the imprisonment of five of Von Bork's most skillful agents and the blunting of his nefarious plans.

It was now August 1914—the date preselected by Von Bork as the combination for his safe, which contained his most precious intelligence documents. The crisis was fast approaching, not only for Holmes and Von Bork but for the European world, for the events of that month would effectively end, for good or ill, the nineteenth century which had already extended fourteen years beyond its chronological entitlement.

The time was exactly nine in the evening, the date was August 2, 1914. By noon of the previous day, Russia and Germany were at war. On August 3, Germany would declare war on France, and, on August 4, England would enter the conflagration and lose an entire generation of its best young men.

Baron Von Herling, the chief secretary of the German Embassy, had come in his 100 h.p. Benz touring car for a final visit in England with Von Bork at the latter's country home.

> Above, the stars were shining brightly, and below, the lights of the shipping glimmered in the bay. The two famous Germans stood beside the stone parapet of the garden walk, with the long, low, heavily gabled house behind them, and they looked down upon the broad sweep of the beach at the foot of the great chalk cliff on which Von Bork, like some wandering eagle, had perched himself four years before.

As the Baron was leaving, he observed, "Those are the lights of Harwich, I suppose."

Those geographical clues which Watson (or whoever wrote *His Last Bow*) provides do place the house on the coast, on a high chalk cliff from which the lights of Harwich may be seen. It is outside of a town, as the embassy Benz was blocking the country lane to the house, and near a village, as it was there that it passed the oncoming Ford carrying Holmes and Watson.

Our problem was first to locate the general area of the villa. The reference to the lights of Harwich had to be the starting point. There was no reason for any Watsonian dissembling here, and, like Heinrich Schliemann seeking Troy through the *Iliad,* we had to start with a belief in the historicity of the Canon. Our Troy thus had to be within an eye-view of Harwich.

The blessed English Ordnance Survey maps, the finest of their kind, are a research tool without equal in matters Sherlockian. No more than a cursory examination was necessary to establish from the land configurations that the Von Bork villa had to be south of Harwich.

Approximately four miles south of Harwich and across the bay is the Naze, a promontory by which are located two seaside resorts, Walton-on-the-Naze and its more elegant southerly neighbor, Frinton-on-Sea, near to which Holmes had

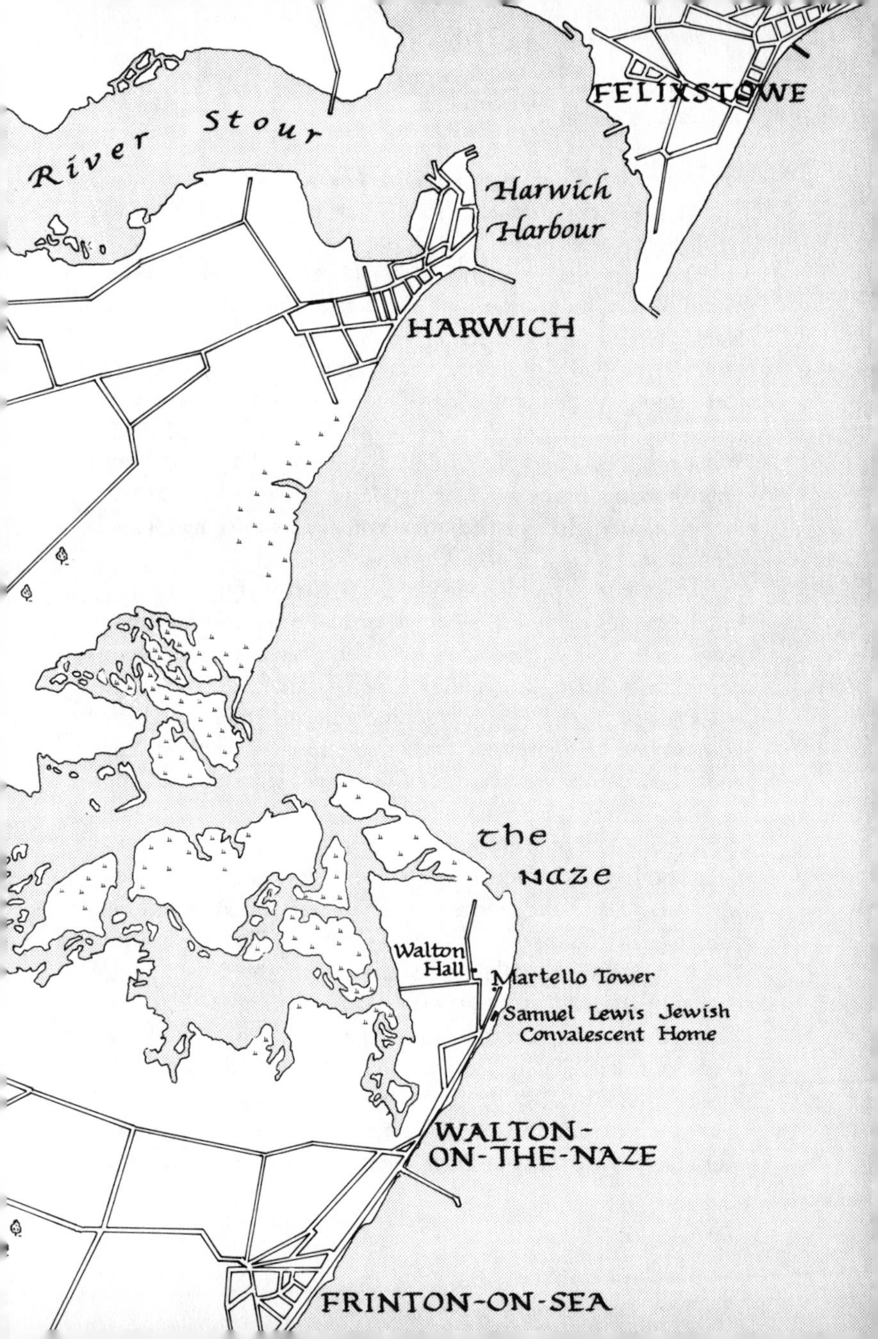
FELIXSTOWE
River Stour
Harwich Harbour
HARWICH
the Naze
Walton Hall
Martello Tower
Samuel Lewis Jewish Convalescent Home
WALTON-ON-THE-NAZE
FRINTON-ON-SEA

once decoyed Josiah Amberley in *The Retired Colourman*. The area westerly from the Naze is low ground and contains no cliffs.

The particular Ordnance map of this region showed an estate a few miles north of Walton-on-the-Naze, toward Harwich, and near the center of the Naze, a protuberance originally called "the nose" and long since linguistically corrupted. The manor was identified as Walton Hall, the sole estate on the Naze and situated in a sparsely settled area. What could be a better location for Von Bork than a secluded English manor house overlooking Harwich and its bay? I went to bed that night satisfied that Von Bork's villa had been identified.

It was late September when we arrived in Essex, having hired a car at Colchester, to which we had come by train from London. Britrail, British Railways, offers a rather fine package, not that expensive, which is ideal for the canonical traveler. It is a two- or three-week pass, obtainable in America, which permits one to ride either first or second class on the trains and to have unlimited car rental at various stations from the firm of Godfrey Davis.

Essex is east of London and on the North Sea. It is low-lying and level, with a just reputation for its oysters. It is laced with tidal creeks and smells untidily of the sea. After a fish-and-chips (a disappearing cuisine) stop in Walton-on-the-Naze, we drove a mile directly north to the Naze, and, honoring the PRIVATE ROAD signs by stopping the car, we tramped on until, through the trees on the west side of the road, we spied the chimneys of what had been Walton Hall. It was soon obvious that it had been a mouldering ruin, settling slowly into the earth, for many years before Von Bork ever graced the county of Essex. Its precincts were surrounded by old barns and cattlesheds, sentinels which ignored its existence. There was no parapet, nor did it front the sea, and by no stretch of architectural imagination could it be described as low and heavily gabled. It was fake brick—Gothic in execution, and its lines were vertical rather than horizontal. There was no compromising with integrity—it was not the villa.

There were other estates along the backwaters, and dejectedly we drove along the southern and western water edge, seeing in turn Marsh House, Birch Hall, Landermere Hall, and both new and old Moze Halls, but none possessed the Von Borkian ambience, nor did any meet Watson's spare description.

By now it was very late in the afternoon, and we could have been no more discouraged had we been wandering with Moses in the desert. We had seen a Martello Tower on our way to Walton Hall, one of those curious round towers built by Pitt along the south and east coasts of England during the fear of the Napoleonic invasions, and, wishing to examine it, we decided to return there and defer the problem.

Where was the aquiline Von Bork's country home? If the canonical references are geographically accurate, it would be in Essex. There have been doubters. Gordon Sewell's work entitled *Holmes and Watson in the South Country* is quoted by Baring-Gould as discounting Dover as too conspicuous and Cornwall as too remote but proposing a location somewhere near Portland and Portsmouth and, specifically, remote Studland, on the Hampshire peninsula known as the Isle of Purbeck, west of the Isle of Wight on England's Channel coast. To adopt this attribution would require a complete repudiation of the canonical reference to the lights of Harwich. It is true that Watson dissembles geographically, but only in the interest of avoiding injury to the innocent, and there were no innocents in *His Last Bow.* An identification of the spy Von Bork's home would in no way embarrass anyone.

If geographical subterfuge is unnecessary and unreasonable, then an incorrect appellation would arise only by the frailty of recollection. Surely even Watsonian vagaries from advancing age would fall far short of failing to recall the dramatic events of their last case together and, as Holmes prophesied, perhaps their final meeting.

There is another less tangible clue indicating the English coast by the North Sea. As Holmes and Watson were leaving, Holmes pointed back to the moonlit sea and shook a thoughtful head.

"There's an east wind coming, Watson."

"I think not, Holmes. It is very warm."

But Holmes was speaking metaphorically, and the east wind was the imminent German onslaught. Referring as it did to Germany, such a wind would have geographical reasonableness in Essex but not in southern Hampshire.

Michael Harrison is convinced that the Von Bork villa was on the east coast, but he correctly notes that there are no great chalk cliffs around Harwich Bay. To be able to view with care the Harwich area would be a decided advantage for a spy who, among other things, was interested in naval matters.

The Martello Tower was no different from the others we had seen and was located at the northern limits of Walton-on-the-Naze and hard by the coast. As we were walking back to the car, we noticed the first structure south of the tower, one which faced the sea and appeared to be long, low, and heavily gabled. It *had* to have been Von Bork's residence. Inquiry from persons walking along the bluffs quickly dis-

The villa of the Kaiser's spymaster Von Bork—"long, low, heavily gabled," and overlooking the harbor at Harwich—was converted into a Jewish convalescent home after the outbreak of the World War in 1914. The structure was torn down shortly after this photograph was taken.

closed that it was the Samuel Lewis Jewish Convalescent Home, vacant and soon to be demolished.

The Lewis structure was built in 1910, in the fullness of the Edwardian age, complete with six large gables and satisfying the requirements of being both low and long. "Heavily gabled" is an appropriate description of the building, and Watson, as usual, captured the flavor of the house in a short and trenchant phrase. It fronts the sea and is some fifty feet above it. True, the cliffs are not chalk but sandstone and limestone, but one cannot fault Watson for a lack of geological insight. It is the kind of structure in which Von Bork would find those heavy comforts so important and familiar to a German nobleman. Unfortunately, the local folk with whom we talked advised that the building was constructed as a convalescent home and always had been used as such. While oral tradition is often a significant guide to Holmesian locations, it must not be uncritically accepted. Two German wars are difficult for the British to forget, and the inhabitants of Walton-on-the-Naze are to be forgiven for their evident reluctance to acknowledge that one of the most masterly of all German spies resided in their precincts during 1910–14 as a respected citizen. The residences of Lord Haw-Haw and General Arnold in Britain and America, respectively, are not accorded great recognition by their neighbors and possess no brass plaques.

The logic of the situation suggests that Von Bork selected a site overlooking the port of Harwich, which is also a naval base, not neglecting a comfortable location for the erection of a mansion, and that he did so in 1910, a canonical date. This is the very year the Lewis establishment was constructed, as the date on the building attested, and the concatention of circumstances would have been sufficient for even Holmes himself. Watson described the home sparingly but adequately.

So it was here that the last recorded exploit of our two aging co-adventurers occurred. It was here that they savored Von Bork's precious golden imperial Tokay from the cellars of Emperor Franz Josef, who had once sent a case to Queen Victoria as a Jubilee gift, a gift regarded as a most appropriate and suitable recognition between sovereigns.

Holmes, who once preferred Montrachet, itself a respected vintage, accorded to himself a toast in one of the world's most unattainable wines. It was a proper vintage with which to offer a liquid commemoration to the end of their long and adventurous association.

There was a cold wind from the North Sea blowing for us too, and, satisfied that we had located the site of Holmes's last encounter, we turned back to the inn for our own celebration with an ample sufficiency of gin and tonics before dinner. We had booked (as the British say) accommodations at one of those delightful English inns, this one not as old as Beowulf, and indeed late Edwardian, but overlooking the North Sea from the rather posh garden resort of Frinton-on-Sea. It was the Maplin Hotel, not an elegant but a comfortable hostelry with all activity revolving, English fashion, from the tap room for a before-dinner drink or two, to the dining room, afterward to the drawing room for coffee and liqueurs. Naturally, each of these rooms overlooked the sea.

It would have been pleasant to make a short side trip to Little Purlington, "near Frinton," which had seemed to Watson to be "the most primitive village in England" and where the long-suffering doctor and client Josiah Amberley were forced to spend a night at the Railway Arms during the investigation of *The Retired Colourman.* We might have sought the hotel and the vicarage of J. C. Elman, the ill-humored incumbant of Mossmoor-cum-Little Purlington, but again there is no Mossmoor, no Little Purlington, no Railway Arms, nor were there in 1898, the year of that adventure.

Dinner for us was at seven that evening, as we were leaving early the next morning for Norfolk in search of Donnithorpe, where Holmes stayed with the Trevors during the long vacation sometime between the years 1872 and 1876, and where he first evidenced those superb ratiocinative powers of his.

Many pleasant winter evenings had been spent in my study, poring over maps of Norfolk, searching for the nonexistent village of Donnithorpe. In the northwestern corner of county Norfolk there was a village which, on a trial basis, could be Donnithorpe's surrogate, but, aside from this rather tenuous connection, there was little to go on, and Norfolk is a big county. Over after-dinner coffee in the comfortable drawing room of the Maplin, I had my worn Ordnance surveys of Norfolk spread out, an almost inevitable invitation to an Englishman to overcome his privacy resolve. Within minutes, a friendly fellow guest from Norfolk inquired as to the purpose of my search, and I shared my problem. Now, Sherlock Holmes is a serious non-literary figure in Britain, and inquiry into matters connected with him are not taken lightly. My fellow guest was extremely helpful and furnished a significant and vital bit of information which narrowed the search for Donnithorpe to manageable proportions. It was information familiar to Norfolk natives and probably to Britons in general—that the Broads, where Holmes enjoyed wild-duck shooting and "remarkably good" fishing during his stay with the Trevors, constitutes a significant but precise portion of Norfolk. They are nowhere near the northwestern part of the county, where my map research had taken me.

The rest of that evening involved a further review of the Canon, which vouchsafed geographically only that Donnithorpe was "a little hamlet just to the north of Langmere, in the country of the Broads. The house was an old-fashioned, widespread, oak-beamed brick building, with a fine lime-lined avenue leading up to it." It had high chimneys and a flagpole. The place afforded superb fishing and duck hunting in the fens, and Trevor had a boat.

There is no Langmere in the entire county of Norfolk, and of course there is no Donnithorpe. Shell's *English Motorist's Atlas* does list a Langham, which is located about five miles

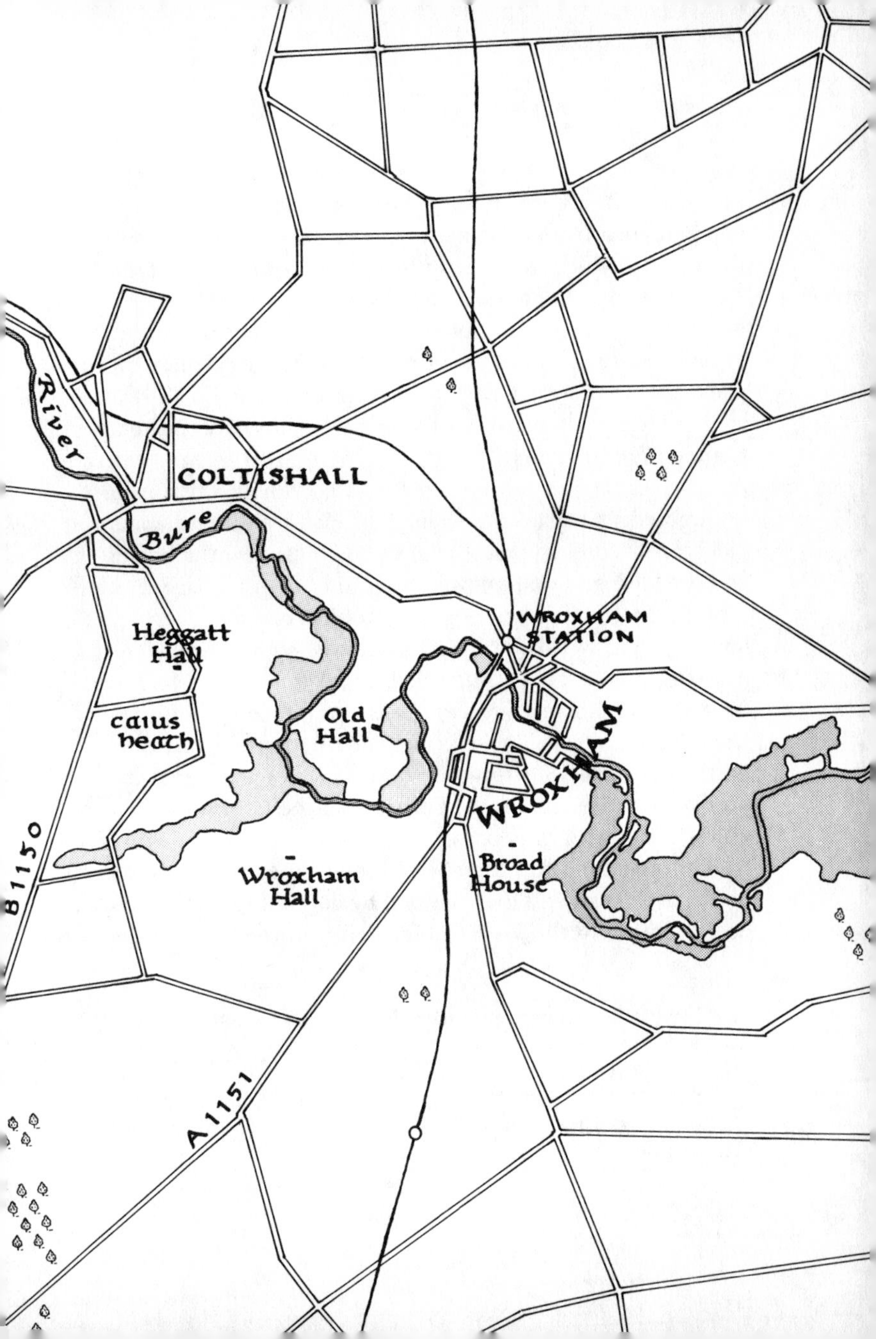

River
COLTISHALL
Bure
WROXHAM STATION
Heggatt Hall
caius heath
Old Hall
WROXHAM
B1150
Wroxham Hall
Broad House
A1151

from the north coast, which had been my original thought, but, since I now knew that the Norfolk Broads is a distinctive and particular region, Holmes's allusion, not to the *county* of the Broads, which would refer to Norfolk county, but to the *country* of the Broads, was determinative of the issue. The reference is clearly to the Broads, which the maps showed to be an area including and surrounding the River Bure and particularly the area of Coltishall to Barton Common. It is an area of fens and marshes—a watery paradise for boaters, hunters, and fishermen.

The Langmere allusion being an evident misnomer, undoubtedly to spare the feelings of Holmes's friend about old Trevor's criminal past, the town had to be near the Broads and it had to be a well-known town rather than a village, as it is proffered as the identifying geographical feature. There are few large and well-known Norfolk towns, with the only one near the Broads being Norwich,* the county seat. "Just to the north" of Norwich are two towns in the Broads, Coltishall and Wroxham, with the latter being more northeasterly than north, but each lying approximately six miles away from the present Norwich city limits. Both are on the rail line, and it was by rail that Holmes arrived.

On his second trip there, Holmes was met at the station by young Trevor, and they traveled by dog cart (a small, one-horse vehicle) to the Trevor home. They hurried "along the

*There would seem to be no clear linguistic transference between Langmere and Norwich, other than that both are descriptive geographical terms. According to the *Oxford Universal Dictionary,* the former means a sheet of standing water and the latter is a compound word for a salt-making town with the Middle English abbreviation of north.

On the Broads of Norfolk

smooth white county road, with the long stretch of the Broads in front of us glimmering in the red light of the setting sun. From a grove upon our left I could already see the high chimneys and the flagstaff which marked the squire's dwelling."

We arrived at Norwich by rail early the next morning and immediately left by rented car to cover the few miles to Wroxham. The wan, late-September sun warmed the low, flat Norfolk countryside, which looked clean and prosperous. It's a clear, bright county, and there is little rainfall but much surface water, with many slow-moving rivers, the Broads—which are really connected waterways surrounded by marshland and pierced by canals and embanked rivers—and of course the North Sea, which touches two sides of the county. There are many woods in this part of Norfolk which effectively act as sentinels of privacy. South of Wroxham, a charming village dominated by water recreation, we started examining the possible sites marked on our Ordnance map, checking off Wroxham Hall, Broad House, and Old Hall. That left the area around Coltishall to the west. We noted with satisfaction that a rail line extended beyond Wroxham Station a short distance north of Coltishall. Holmes had been met at the station by young Trevor, and on the way to the house "the long stretch of the Broads was in front . . . glimmering in the red light of the setting sun." Holmes does not state in which direction they went, but the impression is westward, or at least it was for me initially, but a careful reading does not confirm this. They could easily have gone south and seen the Broads reddened by the sunset. If they had taken, as we did, what is now B1150 for some two miles, turning left, or eastward, at the Caius Heath intersection, they would have seen, as Holmes related, high chimneys above a grove of trees to their left, which was Squire Trevor's dwelling.†

This is Heggatt Hall, which is entered, as in the adventure, through an avenue of trees, although not limes, but one of the distinguishing characteristics of the house is its chimneys. While it is not entirely red brick, yet it is extensively and elaborately trimmed in such brick and is otherwise flint; its ambience is red brick, however, and it is not surprising that it would be so marked and remembered.

I could see, through the thick band of trees bordering the easterly road, the main features of the Hall, just described,

---

†There is a problem, for there is a shorter road from Coltishall along the east of the dwelling. Holmes could have mistaken left for right when he related the story many years later to Watson, or he could have been taken over B1150, which is a much better road.

The Trevor estate near Donnithorpe, where Holmes's first case occurred

and yearned for a closer look. I was reluctant to trespass, though, as the English cherish their privacy and, for perhaps the same reason, their hedges, and are prone to be very reserved with strangers. Introductions, socially unnecessary in a frontier America, are important in England. I did not wish to be an intruder, but Audrey finally stopped my roadside pacing with a reminder that I had come a long way to see such sights. Suitably emboldened, I walked down the tree-girt entranceway and ran into Mrs. R. E. F. Gurney, the owner's wife, a very pleasant young lady, and soon after Mr. Gurney joined us in his Wellington boots, fresh from overseeing the reroofing of one of the estate buildings. They were most polite but, never having read the Holmes stories, were just a shade doubtful about my *bona fides.* Nonetheless, they permitted me to view and photograph the exterior of their home and the grounds.

Heggatt Hall is a T-shaped dwelling, with the top of the T facing the east. It is Jacobean, with several stepped gable ends, three stories in height, and with elaborate brickwork—altogether a very attractive residence, set in pleasant grounds. It is still a working estate. The entrance to the house is to the east, but it also faces south, where there is a lawn and croquet yard. It was in this area to the south that the two Trevors and Holmes were sitting in garden chairs when the sinister seaman Hudson arrived to the evident discomfiture of the elder Trevor. Hudson was what the Austrians call a *pechvogel,* a bird of misfortune, whose prey in this case was old Trevor himself.

If indeed Squire Trevor was a predecessor in title to Heggatt Hall, the fact that the Gurneys were not readers of the Canon is the type of mild irony which Holmes would have appreciated.

* * *

Flushed with the success of our two East Coast identifications, we were ready to relax a bit and confirm the previously-made identifications, both in the county of Norfolk and both involving *The Dancing Men,* one of Conan Doyle's favorites, he having listed it as the third best of the Holmes stories. Perhaps on a more subtle level, his preference may have been influenced by his personal distaste for Holmes and his preference for his other creation, Professor Challenger, for, in *The Dancing Men,* Holmes had one of his rare failures—the death of his client. He did not save Hilton Cubitt, whom he was able only to avenge, not a very salutary result.

The adventure occurred in late July of either 1888 or 1898, depending upon which Jubilee is accepted as the measuring year. All commentators, without exception, accept the latter date, but surely the internal evidence favors the earlier, for had both Jubilees occurred Cubitt would have specified to which he was alluding. Since he referred only to "the Jubilee," it had to be the first, in 1888.

The Cubitt family had been at their seat of Ridling Thorpe for five hundred years. They were a well-known, respected family, and Hilton Cubitt was the last of their line. There is some confusion as to whether the estate was known as Riding Thorpe or Ridling Thorpe. Doubleday's *The Complete Sherlock Holmes* uses the former, while English editions state the latter. According to D. Martin Dakin, the initial reference in the *Strand* magazine was to Riding, but thereafter it was designated as Ridling. As there is a small town called Ridlington near the area where the Manor was apparently located, it is likely that the correct name is Ridling Thorpe and the first mention in the *Strand* was a compositor's error which has been perpetuated in the American editions of the Canon.

Watson is unusually specific as to the location of the Manor. He states that it was seven miles from North Walsham and within sight of the North Sea, with the village of East Ruston some miles off. North Walsham is five miles from the Norfolk coast, so the direction of the Manor, situated as it was within sight of the coast, must be two miles farther on. There is evidence extrinsic to the Canon strongly pointing to the area around Happisburgh, on the coast, which is some seven miles from North Walsham and about two miles from Ridlington.

John Dickson Carr, in his excellent biography of Conan

Doyle, relates the genesis of the idea of *The Dancing Men*. According to Carr, Doyle was staying at the Hill House Hotel at Happisburgh (pronounced *haysboro*) while on a motoring holiday in 1903. The hotel was operated by a family named Cubitt, and their small son was in the habit of writing his name in a code of dancing men. Carr also relates that Doyle wrote the story in the Green Room of the Hill House Hotel, which was on the water side of the hotel overlooking the bowling green.

It was a bright, chilly autumn afternoon when we arrived at Happisburgh, more than an hour's drive from Norwich. Happisburgh is a small hamlet on the brink of the North Sea. Trees are a bit more spare and twisted here than on the Broads, and it is sandier, and a strong wind blows in from the sea.

Hill House, where Sir Arthur Conan Doyle was inspired to write the adventure of *The Dancing Men* in 1903. The pub is still in business at left, but the former hotel, the three-story structure on the right, is now a private residence.

Hill House as viewed from the North Sea shore. The Green Room in which Doyle actually wrote *The Dancing Men* is beyond the windows of the first (American second) floor where a light can be seen burning.

Hill House draws its name from a rather tame hill hard by the ocean's shingle. The exterior structure of the Hill House Hotel still remains—a rambling, whitewashed brick building with red-tiled roofs at various heights. It is indistinguishable from any other similar establishment, except perhaps for the roofs, which are a bit too tropical for Norfolk. All that survives of the original hotel is the pub. Knowing that the quickest, if the least authoritative, source of information is the village tavern, I entered the Hill House, while Audrey, weary of pubs, waited in the car.

The matronly operator of the pub spoke with some feeling about the landlord no longer leasing to her the hotel portion of the building. That is the three-story portion which contained the Green Room where Doyle wrote *The Dancing Men.* It is now a private residence, but the pub continues to offer libations to the weary traveler and thirsty locals alike. When I explained to her the purpose of my search, she recalled that a few years ago a very tall, elderly man came to the Hill House and confided that he was the young Cubitt whose parents had once operated the hotel and whose code of dancing men had so intrigued Conan Doyle. There is a framed newspaper clipping commemorating Mr. Cubitt's sentimental journey in search of his youth.

Where was Ridling Thorpe Manor? None of the locals, helpful as they were, could furnish any assistance as to the prototype of the Manor. The canonical description is sparse, only that "two old brick and timber gables projected from a grove of trees" and that "there was a porticoed front door." Baring-Gould has written that Miss Shirley Sanderson has identified it as Walcott House. Reference to the particular Ordnance Survey map relating to the area evidenced only three possibilities, all approximately one mile from Ridlington and two miles from East Ruston: East Ruston Hall, Walcott Hall, and Walcott House. We drove the short distance to view all three. The first two may be summarily dismissed, as neither East Ruston Hall nor Walcott Hall possesses any gables.

Walcott House has four gables, which is not an insurmountable obstacle as Watson may have missed two of them (after all, they projected from a grove of trees) or even forgotten them. A more serious problem is that the gables are not brick and timber but small and set in the roof. Walcott

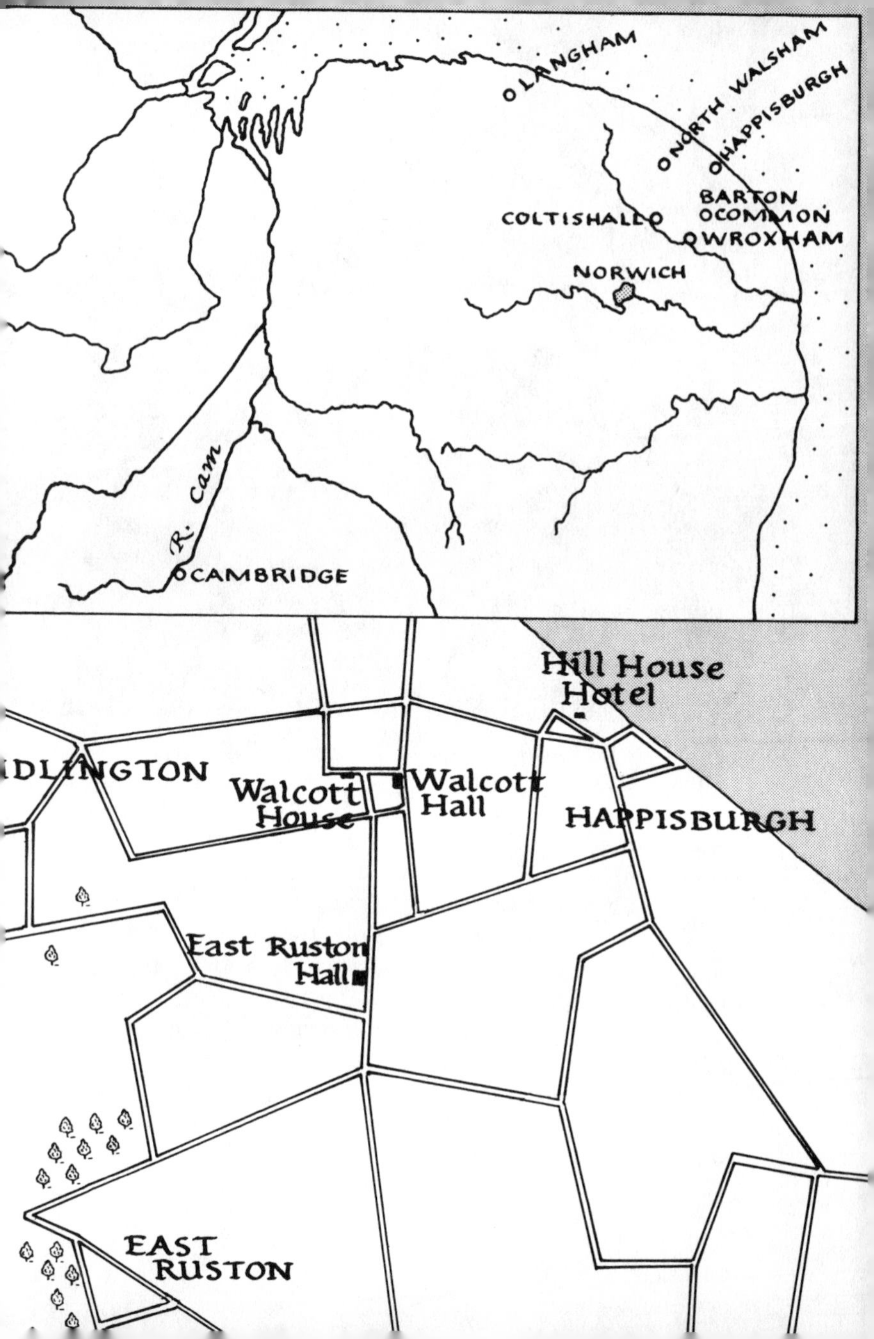
LANGHAM
NORTH WALSHAM
HAPPISBURGH
BARTON
COMMON
COLTISHALL
WROXHAM
NORWICH
R. Cam
CAMBRIDGE
Hill House
Hotel
IDLINGTON
Walcott
House
Walcott
Hall
HAPPISBURGH
East Ruston
Hall
EAST
RUSTON

Ridling Thorpe Manor

House is a red-brick, three-storied dwelling, with the third floor being represented by the four dormers. It is not possible to view the North Sea from the grounds, though the Martello Tower at the edge of the ocean is observable. Even though there are some difficulties of correspondence between the canonical description and the home itself, Walcott House remains the most likely site of the star-crossed and ill-fated Cubitts.

All in all, it was a most fruitful East Anglian adventure, and my wife felt on more than one occasion that she heard some spectral Holmes murmur, "Capital, capital."

XII. Cambridge and Trumpington

THREE of the canonical adventures—*The Three Students, The Creeping Man,* and *The Missing Three-Quarter*—are set in celebrated university towns. There has been much learned speculation by Holmesian scholars as to whether the three students attended Cambridge or Oxford, and at which of the two universities it was that Professor Presbury taught when not ascending the outsides of its buildings. The "Camford" to which the professor was attached and the identification of the academic fount at which two at least of the three students drank is subject to dispute, but there is no dispute as to which school *The Missing Three-Quarter* belonged.

That adventure is replete with clear and unambiguous references to Cambridge, and it was to Cambridge, then, in February, probably of 1897, that the two Holmes-described "middle-aged London gentlemen" traveled to seek the elusive Godfrey Staunton, the missing Rugby three-quarter. They commenced their investigation at the home of Dr. Leslie Armstrong, one of the heads of the school of medicine and a thinker of Continental renown, who resided in "a large mansion on the busiest thoroughfare." After the resolute Dr. Armstrong had them peremptorily removed, they repaired to the "little inn just opposite Armstrong's house," which Holmes concluded was "singularly adapted to our needs," securing a room facing the street.

So much for the verities of the Canon. It seemed so simple

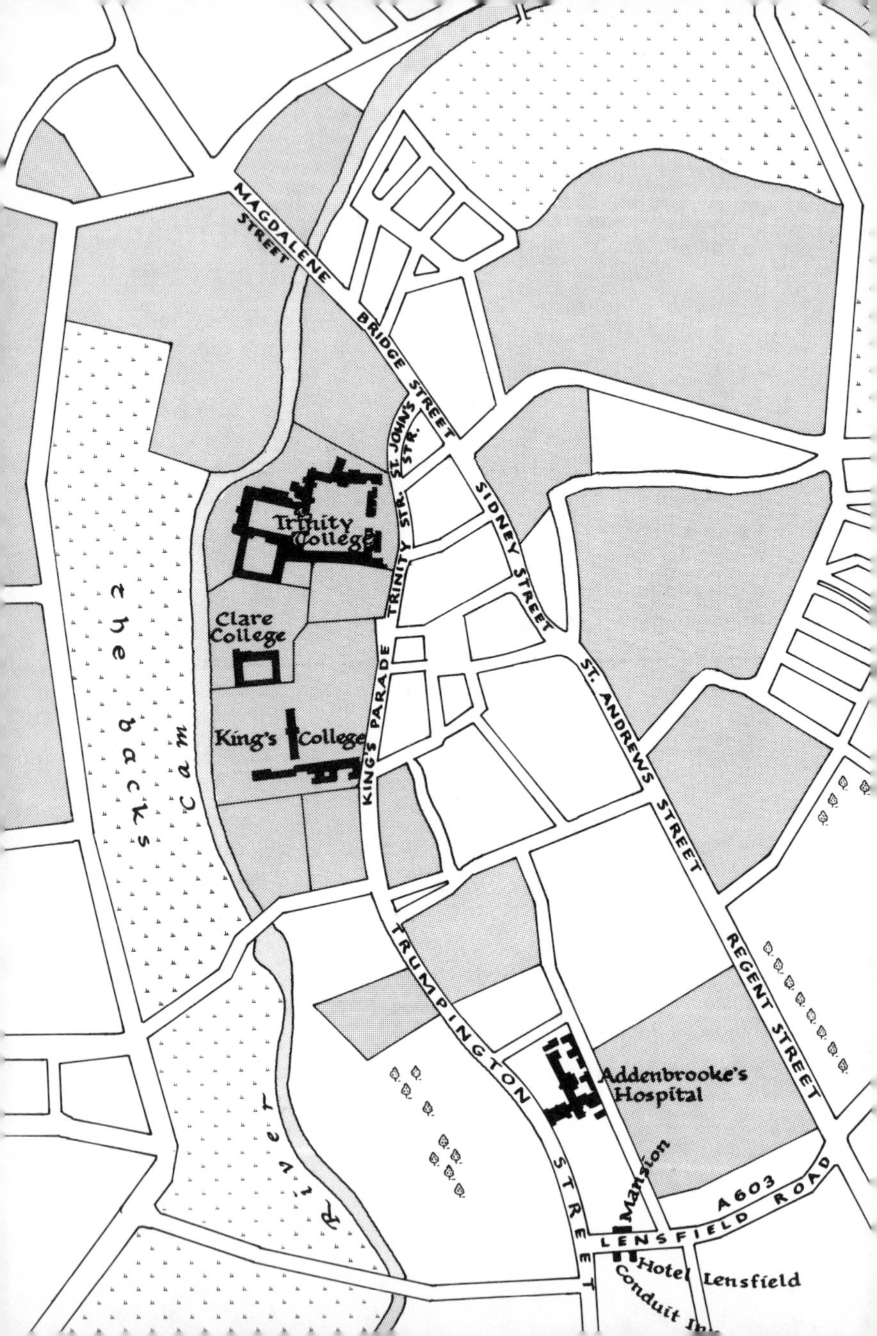

MAGDALENE STREET
BRIDGE STREET
ST. JOHN'S STR.
SIDNEY STREET
TRINITY STR.
Trinity College
Clare College
King's College
KING'S PARADE
ST. ANDREWS STREET
the backs
Cam
TRUMPINGTON STREET
REGENT STREET
Addenbrooke's Hospital
River
Mansion
A603
LENSFIELD ROAD
Hotel Lensfield
Conduit In

on those winter evenings back home: Look for the busiest thoroughfare, find a mansion across from a hotel, and there you are, a definitive attribution. We were so certain of the ease of selection that we took a day train from London to Cambridge, intending to be back no later than midafternoon, but there is something about Holmesian research which quickly confounds the most optimistic hopes and speedily dashes them.

Cambridge, some fifty miles north of London, is the center of almost 100,000 in population lying in the area known as The Fens, which is a low-lying land, once marshland before drainage. Its downtown, the "town centre" as the British describe it, is like that of any other town except for the University, most parts of which are sprinkled in and around the town centre.

The "busiest thoroughfare" of Cambridge in Holmes's day—in this case, Trumpington Street. The intersection leading to Lensfield Road lies directly behind the photographer.

Where was the "busiest thoroughfare"? The city street plan showed what seemed to be the busiest streets as forming an inverted V. We started our search on foot in a northerly direction on Regent Street near our car park. This street becomes, European-fashion, St. Andrews' Street, then Sidney Street, then Bridge Street where it crosses the river Cam, and then Magdalene (pronounced *maudlin*) Street, and so forth. There were many stores, suitably small according to English preferences, on the left and several venerable college buildings on the right with their cloistered courts, but no large mansions nor any small inns opposite. It was discouraging, but there remained the other arm of the V, and, turning at the apex, we followed the other main thoroughfare, St. John's Street, which bewilderingly became in rapid succession Trinity Street, King's Parade, and finally, with a longer fidelity of distance, Trumpington Street. We made the obligatory tourist stops for the elegant Clare College gateway, four hundred years old and never completed, and the charming King's College Chapel with its lacy stone tracery. The River Cam parallels the street at a discreet distance of a quarter of a mile, along which lay the famous parks known as the Backs. By the time we had passed old Addenbrooke's Hospital, situated near the Lensfield Road crossing, it was apparent that this busy thoroughfare also possessed no mansions with inns across the street. It was a dismal conclusion, but we had run out of busy thoroughfares and it was time to return the car to the railroad station.

While walking along Lensfield Road, we suddenly spied on the north side of the street an elegant mansion, and to the south, across from the mansion, stood not one but two small hotels. Like Keats's Cortez at the Pacific, we gazed with wild surmise.

Dr. Leslie Armstrong's house in Lensfield Road, Cambridge

The mansion was a large and commodious, rectangular, drab-yellow brick structure, three stories in height, with an iron balcony on the first (American second) story, set unusually close to the street. It is Nos. 4 and 5 Benet Place and is close to Addenbrooke's Hospital, an obvious convenience which would have been appealing to a teaching physician who was head of the medical school.

Lensfield Road extends east and west, and across the road from the Benet Place house are two small hotels or inns, the easternmost at No. 53 being the Hotel Lensfield and the westernmost, at No. 61, the Conduit Inn, the original name of which appears in stone on its face—Waterloo House. Both

One of these hotels was the "little inn just opposite" the Armstrong mansion where Holmes and Watson stayed during their search for *The Missing Three-Quarter.* The Hotel Lensfield (left) is the larger, but the Conduit Inn (right) possesses greater appeal for the Sherlockian wayfarer.

inns are small, with the 1980 edition of Michelin listing 29 rooms for the Lensfield and not mentioning the Conduit at all. The Lensfield is the result of the connection of two adjoining buildings, a three-story structure painted incongruously in what Audrey characterized as that peculiar shade of hideous Habsburg ochre, some three windows wide, and a two-story structure which is painted institutional gray, apparently in an over-reaction to the exuberance next door.

The Conduit is far less obtrusive, and indeed contents itself, as the western end of a row of dark-brick, connected buildings, with one mark of individuality, a light blue doorframe. A two-story extension with central bay windows thrusts streetward from the center of the building. The Conduit has very evident similarities in architecture and ambience to the Baker Street houses, and I could be reasonably sure this would be Holmes's selection of an inn, his and Watson's room being on the first (American second) floor of the extension, with the bay window being that through which the detective watched Dr. Armstrong's comings and goings. And if any further evidence is needed, what free-born Englishman could resist an inn called the Waterloo?

Everything seemed so right, yet I remembered the canonical injunction about the "busiest thoroughfare." Lensfield Road was in fact bearing heavy traffic, and a check with the city map established that it connects with both of the streets which we had so discouragingly walked, as well as being the main east-west traffic artery. It also carried Highway A20, going south, and Highway A603 going east and west, and, more importantly, it formed a T intersection less than a hundred feet to the west with Trumpington Street, which is the route to the village of the same name, near which the search for the grieving three-quarter was concluded.

Some years after *The Missing Three-Quarter,* in 1903, Holmes and Watson were obliged to be in "Camford" incident to the case of *The Creeping Man,* and as Holmes then recalled: "There is, if I remember right, an inn called the Chequers where the port used to be above mediocrity and the linen above reproach." These are recommendations of a traveler who has stayed there, one who can speak from personal evaluation. There was not in the 1890s any inn by that name, as a search of the Cambridge street directories confirms, although there is one in what was then Trumpington. There was once a Chequers Inn in a passageway off the High Street in Oxford, but the *situs* of *The Missing Three-Quarter* is clearly and unequivocably Cambridge and Cambridgeshire. Watson could mistake the name of the inn, but it is unlikely that he would fall into error regarding the town and county, all of which indicates that *The Creeping Man* and *The Three Students* may well have occurred in Oxford.

The village of Trumpington referred to by Watson does exist and was some three miles south of Cambridge, but it is now encompassed within the municipal limits. The directions regarding the pursuit are explicitly given and involved a convoluted doubling-back by the secretive Dr. Armstrong. They turned out of the main road into a grass-grown lane.

The village of Trumpington has now been absorbed into the Cambridge municipality, but in 1897 it was a quiet refuge from the bustle of the busy University town.

> Half a mile farther this opened into another broad road, and the trail turned hard to the right in the direction of the town, which we had just quitted. The road took a sweep to the south of the town, and continued in the opposite direction to that in which we started. . . . "This should be the village of Trumpington to the right of us."

Ninety years of municipal change have made Watson's directions inexplicable to today's traveler. It was not possible for us to identify the Staunton cottage, once set in a field somewhere near and to the west of Trumpington.

If the cottage of the consumptive corpse, as Erle Stanley Gardner would probably have it, is not and probably will never be identified, there is good reason to believe that the Armstrong mansion and the small inn have been almost inadvertently rediscovered.

At right: The Peak,
the name given to a range
of hills in Derbyshire,
and to the district
roundabout where
Holmes looked into
the Priory School case

XIII.
The Derbyshire Dukeries

It was the overwrought Thorneycroft Huxtable, M.A., Ph.D., etc., who proffered to Holmes his sole adventure in the Peak District.

Professor Huxtable, of *Huxtable's Sidelights on Horace,* and headmaster of the Priory School, had a rather more serious problem than those mild scholarly afflictions which customarily perturb the educator. Lord Saltire, the ten-year-old son and heir of the Duke of Holdernesse, was missing from the Priory School, an institution whose bestiary of noble sons was acceptably long.

In search of the missing lord, Holmes and Watson left London by train for Derbyshire, arriving at Mackleton Station, whence they traveled to the Priory School, described as being nearby. Michael Harrison has ingeniously identified Mackleton as an amalgam of Matlock and Alfreton and placed Holdernesse Hall on the road between Chesterfield and Bakewell, with the Priory School between Matlock and Clay Cross.

Its easterly geographical position precludes Alfreton's involvement, although Watson is quite capable of inventing a name which is an amalgam of two towns. The practical necessity of the matter is that the rail line terminates at Matlock, which, because of the known general position of the Hall and the Priory School from the map appended to the recital of the adventure, requires that Matlock be Mackleton.

While there are some superficial differences between the English and the American editions, they are not material to the assessment of the locale.

It is dismaying that Holdernesse Hall is described so sparingly. This is, however, consistent with the Watsonian practice of obfuscation. We are told only that there was by it a "low gray village," that a "famous yew avenue" was on the grounds, and that the house possessed a "magnificent Elizabethan doorway." The Holdernesse estate was on the Chesterfield high road, two miles west of an inn which was "forbidding and squalid. . .with the sign of a game-cock above the door," by a church and a few cottages. The hills to the north behind the Hall were "precipitous," and south of the road was the Lower Gill Moor, extending for ten miles and "sloping gradually upward." A rough map is included with the tale, and from the map it is clear that the road to Chesterfield ran in a generally east-west direction and south of the Hall, with the Priory School six miles from the Hall across the moor.

The Ordnance maps, the *Shell Motorist's Atlas,* and the other reference works available established that, although Derbyshire is known as "the dukeries," only two ducal residences are within the area delimited by Watson's map and commentary. These are Haddon Hall, seat of the Duke of Rutland, and Chatsworth, the famous ducal mansion of the Duke of Devonshire.

An application of the canonical descriptions to Haddon Hall and Chatsworth House reveal the following: while Haddon has no adjoining village, Chatsworth has an ample sufficiency, with Edensor to the west, Beeley to the south, and Baslow to the north. Both houses are on roads leading to Chesterfield, but neither is on any road designated as the

Chesterfield high road. Both have hills behind, the hills at Haddon rising three hundred feet and those at Chatsworth two hundred.

Lower Gill Moor is a Watsonian-devised term which has no close counterpart by either house. Haddon has moors extending the requisite distance southward, known as Haddon Fields, and, farther away, Gratton Moor, while Chatsworth does not, its moors being to the east. Haddon's geographical position is consistent with the map, being on the north side of an east-west road, while Chatsworth is east of a north-south road. It is arguable that the northerly entrance to Chatsworth is on an east-west road, which incidentally is the highway to Chesterfield, some five miles distant, but it is on the south rather than the north side of that road. Chatsworth is undeniably on the road to Chesterfield, and the road could be physically described as high, while Haddon is some two miles southwest of Chatsworth and farther removed from Chesterfield. Haddon, however, is situated on a road going to Chesterfield, albeit a less traveled one than that upon which Chatsworth fronts.

The county of Derbyshire is in the northwestern part of England, with the city of Derby being some 130 miles from London on the M1 highway. We arrived in Derby by rail one autumn evening without any hotel reservations or any concern for their lack. But some Chicago-like convention had saturated every hotel and hostelry in Derby and environs, and finally, at 10:00 P.M., with the help of an innovative car-hire clerk, accommodations were found at a small establishment. It was a bit primitive by American standards, but the staff were most pleasant and helpful.

Some time after we retired, there was a knock at the door, and I was asked to go down and see the manager. I refused,

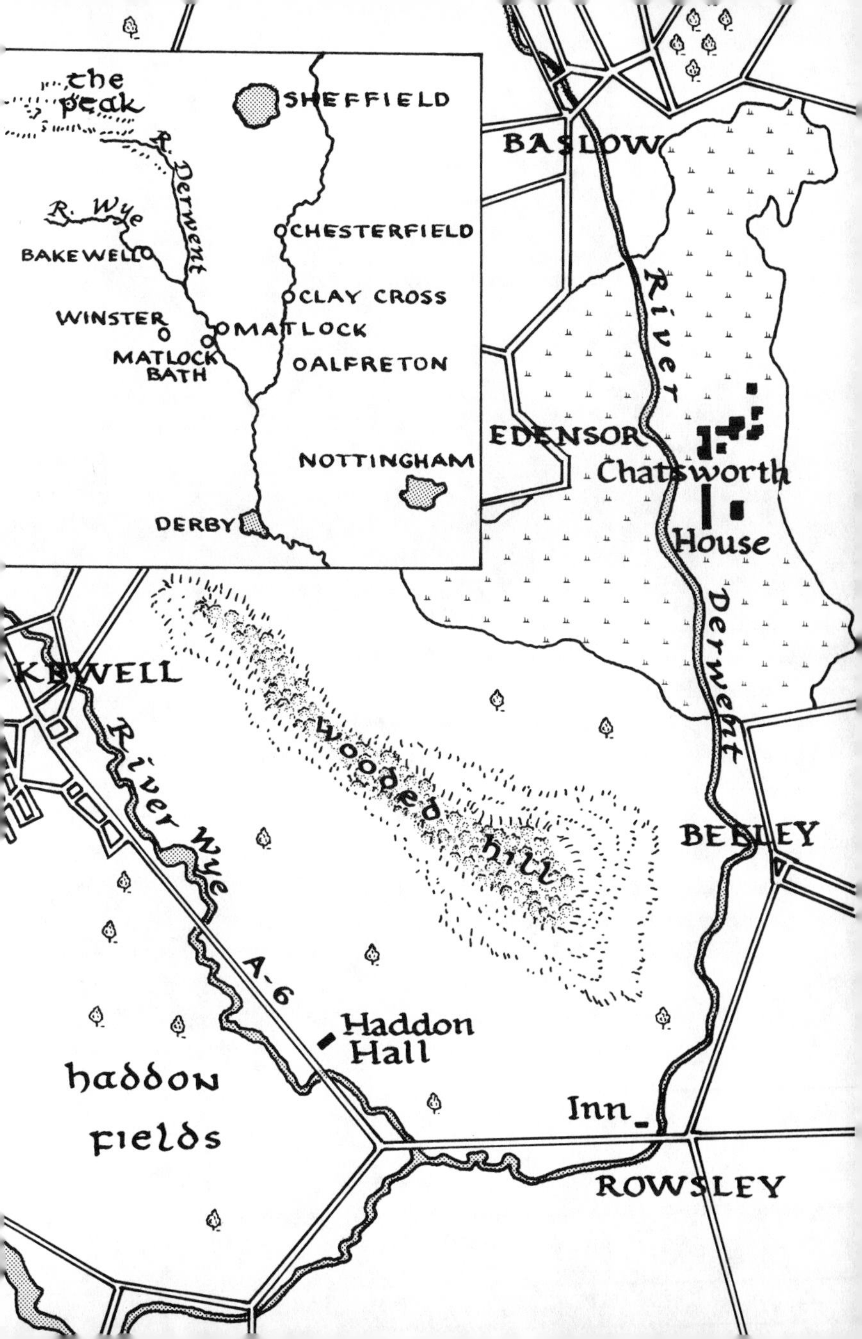

the peak
SHEFFIELD
R. Derwent
R. Wye
CHESTERFIELD
BAKEWELL
CLAY CROSS
WINSTER
MATLOCK
MATLOCK BATH
ALFRETON
NOTTINGHAM
DERBY
BASLOW
River Derwent
EDENSOR
Chatsworth House
KEWELL
River Wye
wooded hill
BEELEY
A-6
Haddon Hall
haddon fields
Inn
ROWSLEY

being dead-tired and thinking it a subterfuge to allow some miscreant to use his cosh on me in the dark and winding hallways. A few minutes later, the knocking started again, with the assurance that indeed it was the manager who required me, so with more than slight trepidation I went, taking a firm grip on my walking stick. The summons arose from the fact that I had told them I would charge the room to my American Express card, and apparently I was the first guest in the hotel's history not to use cash.

Early the next morning, we arrived at Matlock Bath, which was to be our headquarters in the Peak District, finding it an attenuated town following the serpentine valley of the River Derwent. The new Bath Hotel had once been the old Bath Hotel and consisted of a stone building in the Regency style, painted yellow with white trim and quoins, built when Englishmen came here for baths in the warm, restorative mineral waters. A vast new portion was added on when Englishmen began coming here for conventions, but the new Bath Hotel tries very hard not to be institutional.

This part of Derbyshire has soft and gentle hills, with some tree cover. The native dun-colored limestone is used as the building material for almost all the buildings and houses. The towns tend to be folded into the valleys along fiercely-rushing streams. Isaac Walton had a favorite dale nearby, and that is not surprising. To the west are the Peaks, stark and forbidding, but here the landscape is restrained.

Our first stop was Chatsworth, just a few miles up the road. It is easily one of the stateliest of the stately homes of England. This is the mansion which too abundant wealth built. It is a regal showcase—ostentatious, monumental, oversized, and overcivilized. The original house was wholly Elizabethan, having been begun in 1552, but in 1686 the

◂ Holdernesse Hall

fourth Earl and first Duke of Devonshire commenced to transform it into a restrained example of the classic Baroque style of the day, with no Elizabethan vestiges surviving.

Haddon Hall, the other site, was just beyond the hill to the southwest of Chatsworth and southeast of the town of Bakewell, the home of the famous pudding of that name. It is also open to the public. Being a duke does not pay as well as it once did, and admission prices now maintain many manors. Our first view of Haddon Hall was from Highway A6 —a castle rising proudly from the uphill slope of a wooded eminence which reaches to a height of 301 feet. Watson had noted the precipitous hills north behind Holdernesse Hall, and they are both north and steep behind Haddon Hall. According to the good doctor, Lower Gill Moor was south of the road for ten miles, getting gradually higher, and Haddon Fields extend southward from the road and the land does gradually become higher at Gratton Moor.

One enters the grounds on foot through the medieval gatehouse, crossing the River Wye on a substantial stone bridge, and, gradually walking uphill, one reaches the massive and impressive castle. The northwest tower entrance to Haddon's forecourt is Tudor, but not Elizabethan, having been built in 1538. The stables to the left of the entrance are Elizabethan, however, as is the window of the Great Chamber, which is by the entrance to the house itself, and the ambience of a large part of the hall is Elizabethan. No yew walk was found, though the gardens are extensive and well-maintained.

Watson referred to an adjoining village. Bakewell is about a mile west, and Rowsley is about the same distance to the east. Both are tucked in valleys and appear low and gray.

More significantly, Watson mentioned the squalid Fighting Cock Inn as being two miles east of the Hall. There is an inn at Rowsley, though it is neither squalid nor called the Fighting Cock.

There is a subtle but compelling similarity between the names Holdernesse Hall and Haddon Hall, and there are sufficient other parallelisms to permit more than a provisional attribution. The location of the Priory School itself remains elusive, and our time constraints did not permit a search, but, if Watson's map and directions are accurate, it should be along highway A5012, some four miles south of Haddon Hall between Newhaven and Mouldridge Grange, or along the connecting road to Winster from the Grange. And if in your search you meet a German on a bicycle or a horse wearing cloven iron hooves, you know you are hard on the spectral trail from the Priory School to Holdernesse Hall.

At right: The
melancholy Brent Tor,
topped by the church of
St. Michael of the Rock,
was Doctor Watson's
first glimpse of Dartmoor

The West Country

XIV. Dartmoor and the Hound

JAMES MORTIMER, a humble M.R.C.S. of Grimpen, Dartmoor, Devonshire, the self-confessed "picker up of shells on the shores of the great unknown ocean" and owner of a presentation walking stick known as a Penang lawyer, had the temerity to advise Sherlock Holmes that he (Holmes) was the second highest criminal expert in Europe. This is not recommended as the ideal method of attracting the attention of a man who usually preferred a subtle sycophancy, or, at the least, a discreet deference. But Dr. Mortimer's description of Sir Charles Baskerville's dead body in the Yew Alley of Baskerville Hall, with the nearby footprint of an immense hound, redeemed his serious social blunder and afforded readers one of the finest mystery stories in the language.

For the traveling Holmesian, Baskerville Hall is high on the list of sites to explore, and, whatever the disputes regarding its particular location, there is no disputing that the adventure is a West Country one, occurring in the sinister and foreboding desolation known as Dartmoor. Watson's first view of the moor was from the train, the sight of "a gray, melancholy hill, with a strange jagged summit, dim and vague in the distance, like some fantastic landscape in a dream." This has been identified as Brent Tor, and the scene is evocative of the entire adventure, which is bounded and dominated by what Watson called the "ill-omened moor."

The Watson party arrived at an unnamed "small wayside

station" which Baring-Gould has identified as Coryton Station and William H. Gill as either Brent or Ivy Bridge. The three men then progressed in a wagonette by a carefully detailed route to Baskerville Hall, whose grounds were entered through a gateway with two entrance lodges, one a roofless, ruined structure of black granite and the other a new building halfway completed. The Hall itself was reached by a long avenue made dark and menacing by the overhanging trees. Approaching the Hall, Watson observed its central portion, with its porch and thin, twin, ancient, crenellated towers, its high-angled roof and long chimneys, its mullioned windows, and the two modern wings of black granite extending from each side. It had been the seat of the Baskervilles for some five hundred years. Beyond the house was the twelve-foot-high Yew Alley in which Sir Charles had the fatal misfortune to meet his canine nemesis, the apparitional hound. The alley extended from the mansion to a summer house, with a four-foot-high wicket gate opening onto the moor.

Sir Henry was demonstrably moved as he surveyed the ancient and commodious entrance hall, with its high oaken ceiling beams and its twin stairs leading to the gallery. The long dining room, adjacent to the entrance hall, was equally ancient, with a dais for the family, a minstrel gallery, and walls lined with portraits of the ancestral lords of the manor. Here Watson and Sir Henry dined the first night by the feeble light of a shaded table lamp, surrounded by an ominous darkness.

The next morning was warm and clear, restoring Watson's spirits and causing him to walk the "four miles along the edge of the moor. . .to a small gray hamlet, in which two larger buildings, which proved to be the inn and the house of Dr.

Mortimer, stood high above the rest." This was the village of Grimpen, which was located, as Holmes had observed at Baker Street with his Ordnance map before him, fourteen miles from Princetown. It was the hub within a five-mile radius from which were "a very few scattered dwellings," including the Stapletons' Merripit House and Lafter Hall, old Frankland's residence, and "between and around these scattered points extends the desolate, lifeless moor."

The window in the Hall from which Barrymore would return his brother-in-law Selden's signals was a west window which commanded the nearest portion of the moor. Sir Henry and Watson, watching Selden's light, concluded that it was emanating from Cleft Tor, less than one or two miles distant. There is no Cleft Tor on maps of Dartmoor, nor has any resident of the region come forth with information of such a tor. Baring-Gould, whose grandfather, the Rev. Sabine Baring-Gould, was the author of *A Book of Dartmoor* and several other volumes about the region, identifies it as Cleft Rock, which is just above Holne Chase. As a tor means a high rock or pile of rocks, generally on the top of a hill, or a rocky peak, Watson would have been accurate in the use of the term. Cleft Rock, however, must be only a provisional identification.

There is general agreement among Sherlockian scholars that the "small gray hamlet" of Grimpen is Widecombe-in-the-Moor, a delightful little village snugly settled in a valley in the middle of the granite moors. The letter which brought Sir Charles to his appointment with eternity in his own Yew Alley was written by Mrs. Laura Lyons, the estranged daughter of the litigious Frankland of Lafter Hall. She resided in what Watson chose to call Coombe Tracey, identified by Baring-

Gould as Bovey Tracey, which he postulates to be an amalgam of Widecombe and Bovey Tracey.

The Great Grimpen Mire, in which a false step meant "death to man or beast," and into the depths of which the malevolent Stapleton disappeared, has been identified by Michael Harrison as Grimspound Bog, which is on Hameldown Tor, four miles northwest of Widecombe. The Stapletons lived at Merripit House, which Harrison equates with Merrivale and Baring-Gould with Merripit Hill. The home itself has not as yet been identified at either proposed site.

To this day, Baskerville Hall as described by Watson has not been identified. Baring-Gould affectionately, and perhaps

The River Dart, from which Dartmoor takes its name, has its headwaters in the moorland bogs such as the Great Grimpen Mire, as do all the principal streams of Devonshire.

not wholly seriously, presents Lew House, at Lew Trenchard, near Lew Down, Devonshire, as the most likely nominee, and, while it does lack the twin crenellated towers and the massive central portion, there is Lew Wood between the Hall and the moor, which could be what Watson denominated as the Yew Alley. Somewhat more conclusive is the fact that the long-time owners of Lew House had on their coat of arms a bear's head, while on the pillars of the lodge gates of Baskerville Hall were boars' heads. He has more than a clinical interest in the attribution, as it was the home of the Baring-Goulds since 1626. The chief and insurmountable objection is that it is on the wrong side of the moor, and too far from what have been designated as Grimpen Mire, Grimpen, and Cleft Tor. All of the distances furnished by Watson would have to be in substantial error for Lew Trenchard Manor to be Baskerville Hall.

In 1932, *The Hound of the Baskervilles* was filmed by England's Gainsborough Pictures, with the Manor House near Moretonhampstead used as Baskerville Hall. It likewise lacks the slender twin towers, but a more serious objection is that it was not completed until 1907, although its style is Jacobean. Both Lew Trenchard Manor and the Manor House are presently hotels, the former with eight guest rooms and the latter with sixty-nine.

It had been a long winter poring over the British Ordnance Survey's Tourist Map of Dartmoor, fruitlessly trying to locate a tenable Baskerville Hall somewhere within a manageable distance of Widecombe. Now it was time to make an examination *in situ,* and so anxious were we that we entrained for the West Country directly after landing at Heathrow Airport. It was Sunday, September 16, a pleasant late summer day, ideal for the country and ideal for the quest.

The affluent Manor House Hotel at Moretonhampstead was used as Baskerville Hall in the 1932 film version of *The Hound of the Baskervilles.*

Alighting at Exeter, we drove by hired car over the curving road through Moretonhampstead for a quick look at the Manor House Hotel, a resort which accommodates the affluent. It is a beautifully rambling Gothic structure of begrimed stone, satisfying every aesthetic requirement of Baskerville Hall except, as we have said, for the construction date of 1907 which is carved over the entrance gate. Nor have the pseudo-medieval charms of the Manor House been lost on non-Sherlockians, for no less a transient personage than Joachim von Ribbentrop designated this place to be his country seat after England was conquered by Hitler.

It is only a few miles westward to the moors and through them to Widecombe-on-the-Moor, a rustic village nestling among the Dartmoor hills. The whole area constitutes the Dartmoor Forest, which connotes leafy trees closely arched, but Dartmoor is not like that. Its high hills are barren of any trees. There is low, close-growing vegetation such as gorse and furze, and in the wind they billow like low waves. The trees are only in the sheltered areas, clustering in around the base of the sullen and brooding hills. Mankind has been here for a period longer than recorded history: his stone huts and burial cairns extend throughout the moors, and it was in one of these huts that Holmes secreted himself during the Baskerville investigation.

It was dusk when we arrived at the Wooder Manor Hotel, a comfortable inn snuggled against Hameldown Tor and secure in its own grounds. Wooder Manor itself makes some claim to be the original of Baskerville Hall, but the claim is probably commercial and need not be seriously considered. Grimspound Bog, which is locally reported to have swallowed moor ponies, is on Hameldown Tor, and across the small valley eastward from Wooder Manor is Houndtor, and also Great Houndtor, and with these referents it seemed reasonable to search the valley for the Hall.

Excited, I slept little that night and was up early to find Dartmoor satisfyingly mist-filled. Bagpark, the next great house north of Wooder Manor, was the first possibility explored, as were Natsworthy Manor and Heatree House. None were satisfactory. Since knowledgeable Holmesians had regarded Widecombe as Grimpen, it seemed reasonable to extend the search a bit farther. There were few manor houses in the area, with the only real possibility being Leighon, on the opposite side of Houndtor. It turned out to be a much more modern structure and had no canonical pretensions.

It was getting on in the afternoon, and discouragement was lying like a millstone on our spirits when we stopped at the Georgian mansion which is the park information center near Bovey Tracey to inquire as to any local traditions regarding the location of Baskerville Hall.

"The ill-omened moor" ►

Oral tradition should not lightly be disregarded, and such a tradition exists with regard to Baskerville Hall. We learned that it is regarded locally as being Brooke Manor, which is near the town of Buckfastleigh, some few miles south of Widecombe and near Holne Moor and Buckfastleigh Moor. Also according to local tradition, Conan Doyle had been a guest at Brooke Manor.

Sir Henry Baskerville, approaching his ancestral seat with Watson, could have felt no greater anticipation or excitement than we did scurrying along A38. Brooke Manor is situated in a secluded valley reachable by a private road passing through a densely wooded area. It cannot be seen from the high road, and we took the closest farm lane to the west and, descending, came upon Brooke Farm, which is above and a few hundred feet to the north of Brooke House, across a meadow and the stream of the River Mardle. The owners of the farm were a delightful couple, and we were pleased to take tea in their garden overlooking Brooke House.

They confirmed that Mr. Pye, the present owner, preferred his privacy and that it would be an imposition to intrude upon it. We learned from them also that the builder of Brooke, Richard Cabell, had had a fearsome reputation. He died in 1677, and his legend continues unabated. They shared with us Sabine Baring-Gould's *Little Guide to Devonshire,* which states:

> He was the last male of his line and died with such an evil reputation that he was placed with a heavy stone and a sort of penthouse was built over that with iron gratings to prevent his coming up and haunting the neighbourhood. When he died (the story goes) "fiends and black dogs breathing fire raced over Dartmoor and surrounded Brooke, howling."

Assume for the moment that Brooke Manor is Baskerville Hall. How does it square with the factual data specified in the Canon?

Watson's first view of the moor from the train was, as we have seen, of Brent Tor, which is indeed visible from the railway east of Culverlane, the closest stopping point to Brooke Manor, which is approximately eight miles away, an acceptable wagonette ride.

How did Watson describe the route to Baskerville Hall? "In a few minutes we were flying swiftly down the broad, white road," a fair construction of which is that they did not immediately enter the broad road. A ride of a mile and a half from Culverlane in a northwesterly direction would take a traveler to a broad road which is now Highway A38. The "long, gloomy curve of the Moor, broken by the jagged and sinister hills" would have been to the west:

> The wagonette swung round into a side road, and we curved upward through deep lanes worn by centuries of wheels, high banks on either side, heavy with dripping moss and fleshy hart's-tongue ferns. . . . Still steadily rising, we passed over a narrow granite bridge and skirted a noisy stream which gushed swiftly down, foaming and roaring amid the gray boulders. Both road and stream wound up through a valley dense with scrub oak and fir. . . . A steep curve of heath-clad land, an outlying spur of the moor, lay in front of us.

The side road would be the road north of the hamlet of Dean, still a narrow road, which rises steeply from 231 feet at Dean to a height of 955 feet near the Greendown turnoff. The noisy stream could well be the one by Dean Wood, which for a way parallels the road. The moor extends easterly in this area and could with accuracy be described as an outlying spur in front of travelers.

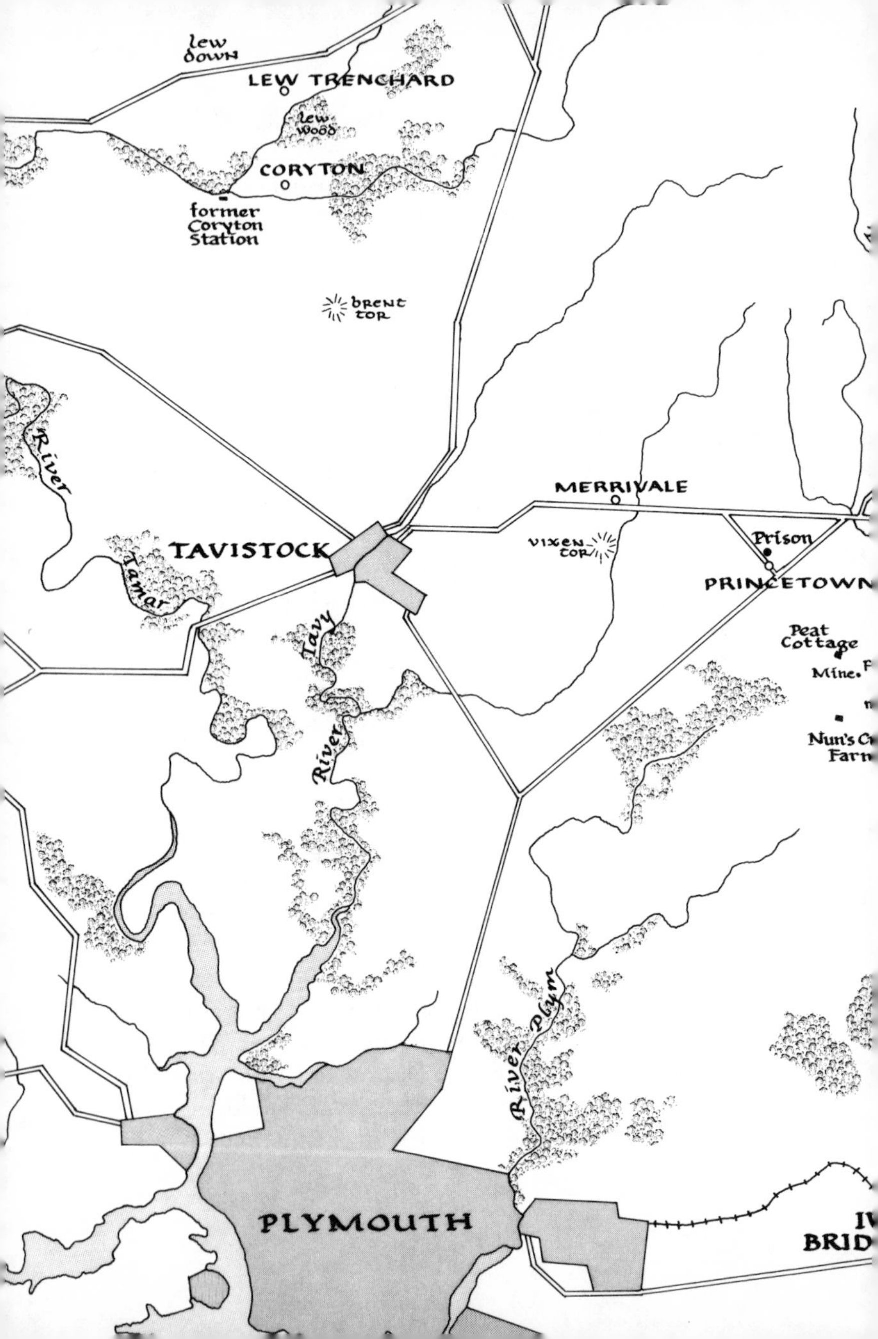
lew down
LEW TRENCHARD
lew wood
CORYTON
former Coryton Station
brent tor
River Tamar
TAVISTOCK
MERRIVALE
vixen tor
Prison
PRINCETOWN
Peat Cottage
Mine.
Tavy
River
River Plym
PLYMOUTH

MORETONHAMPSTEAD
River Teign
Manor House Hotel
River Bovey
grimspound bog
hameldown tor
Heatree House
Natsworthy Manor
greathound tor
hound tor
Leighon Hall
BOVEY TRACEY
Bagpark
Wooder Manor Hotel
WIDECOMBE-IN-THE-MOOR
River
PONSWORTHY
River
Spitchwick Manor
holne chase
A 38
NEWTON ABBOT
holne moor
Hannaford Manor
Snowdown Cairns
Holy Brook
COMBE
River Mardle
pupers hill
Brooke Manor
hickaton hill
BUCKFASTLEIGH
GREENDOWN
dean wood
DEAN
River Dart
black tor
dean moor
White Oxen Manor
Leigh Grange
brent moor
CULVERLANE
POIGNTON
SOUTH BRENT

Our wagonette had topped a rise and in front of us rose the huge expanse of the moor, mottled with gnarled and craggy cairns and tors. . . . The road in front of us grew bleaker and wilder . . . Now and then we passed a moorland cottage . . . Suddenly we looked into a cuplike depression . . . Two high, narrow towers rose above the trees.

The rise would have been the turnoff for Greendown as the road descends from that point to the north. This is moor country and is accurately described by Watson. There are moorland cottages, and the cuplike depression would be the valley formed by the River Mardle, which runs through Brooke Manor.

Watson's route fits neatly with the topography. The problem lies with the physical configurations of Baskerville Hall. Brooke Manor possesses no "two high, narrow towers." It does, however, have two chimneys which taper like towers and from a distance could be the subject of confusion. There are no lodge gates, nor a ruined lodge and new lodge, in fact no lodges at all. The yew alley with the summer home at the end are missing, and the house does not possess twin wings. But it is situated in a "cuplike depression" as described by Watson, with the moor to the west beyond the low hills and fields. We could find no cleft tor within reasonable viewing distance. Pupers Hill, two miles to the west as the crow flies, has a high outcropping which might be where Selden gave his signal, or perhaps it was from Snowdown Cairns, which is about the same distance away from Brooke Manor. These attributions should be tentative until the necessary and obvious tests are performed.

Brooke Manor is smaller than one would imagine Baskerville Hall to be. It is a modified T-shaped structure, with the entrance at the center of the top of the T. It is two stories in

Baskerville Hall

height, with a steeply pitched roof, built of native rubble stone which is ivy-covered in front, with a square, enclosed entrance portico.

The village of Grimpen is stated to be four miles from Baskerville Hall, reachable by a walk along the edge of the moor. Hexworthy is a small hamlet four miles northwest of Brooke Manor and is reachable by a walk along the edge of Holne Moor. When Holmes spread out his Ordnance map, he observed that Grimpen was fourteen miles from Princetown. Widecombe-in-the-Moor is ten miles, and Hexworthy is four miles. The four miles may not be determinative and could well be a printer's error—four instead of fourteen. Hexworthy could still accurately be characterized as a "small gray hamlet." Watson saw two dominant buildings, the inn and

Dr. Mortimer's house, and there is still an inn there. The hamlet huddles in a small valley between the tors formed by the West Dart River.

Where is Grimpen Mire? Local tradition holds it to be the Foxton Mires, still a very deadly place, and located approximately two miles southwest of Hexworthy. Watson, meeting Stapleton at the outskirts of Grimpen, walked with him an unstated distance and, when their paths diverged, accepted Stapleton's invitation to visit Merripit House, which Stapleton observed was "a moderate walk along this moor-path." En route they saw the Great Grimpen Mire in the distance, as well as the stone huts of prehistoric man, which abound in the moor.

Distances in the moors are deceptive. A direct route, as the crow flies, may give little assistance in estimating the distance of travel between points. There are only two main highways through Dartmoor itself, a small scattering of narrower roads, mostly near the perimeter of the moor, and beyond that there are only meandering foot and bridle paths. There are no direct routes, with trails or paths following the time-worn courses of ancient travelers. The moors themselves, except for the incursions of fewer than a handful of dwellings and disused mines of modern man, remain the intact preserve of ancient man. His stone huts, cairns, stone rows, and burial chambers add an ominous and somber note to the stark bleakness. On even the sunniest day, the moor traveler is transported backward thousands of years. It is pleasantly eerie.

Stapleton's reference to a moderate distance could also be deceptive, as the Victorians were inveterate walkers with a greater willingness to walk greater distances. Indeed, Sunday walks remain today an English institution.

After Watson had unexpectedly met Beryl Stapleton, while Jack Stapleton was off chasing a Cyclopides, "a short walk" brought them to Merripit House, "a bleak moorland house, once the farm of some grazier." The view from its windows revealed "the interminable granite-flecked moor rolling unbroken to the farthest horizon." Three-quarters of a mile southwest of the Foxton Mires is Nun's Cross Farm, which is completely surrounded by moor and is accurately described by Watson. Except for nearby Peat Cottage, it is the only home for several miles around.

On a "bog-girt island" in the mire, where the hound was kept, there was an abandoned tin mine, and within a quarter of a mile of the Foxton Mires there is in fact a disused mine.

Wild moor ponies forage by the ruins of Merripit House, where Stapleton prepared his crimes against the Baskervilles.

There is a reasonably direct path from Nun's Cross Farm to Brooke Manor extending some eight miles along the meandering moor paths, an hour and three-quarters' walk, not a substantial one by moor standards. Nun's Cross Farm is also reachable by a path from Hexworthy, and by a road from Princetown to the northwest.

One of the interesting but incidental characters in *The Hound of the Baskervilles* was Frankland of Lafter Hall, a litigious old party who enjoyed asserting long dormant rights. He was "learned in old manorial and communal rights," Watson wrote to Holmes, "and he applies his knowledge sometimes in favour of the villagers of Fernworthy and sometimes against them, so that he is periodically either carried in triumph down the village street or else burned in effigy, according to his latest exploit." Lafter Hall was "some four miles to the south" of Baskerville Hall. If distance and direction are each accurate, Lafter Hall would be near Culverlane, and Leigh Grange or White Oxen Manor would appear likely candidates. The canonical reference to Fernworthy indicated to us that Watson may have erred directionally. Fernworthy is an obvious substitute for either Hexworthy or Ponsworthy. If the identification of Hexworthy as the original of Grimpen is accurate, then Ponsworthy would have been the original of Fernworthy. Some six miles northwest of Brooke Manor and just north of Hexworthy, and two miles west of Ponsworthy, is Laughter Tor, which bears an obvious homonymic relation to Lafter Hall. Between Ponsworthy and Brooke Manor are Spitchwick Manor and Hannaford Manor, each of which is some four miles north from Brooke Manor by road.

Coombe Tracey, the home of Laura Lyons, Frankland's wayward daughter, cannot be Bovey Tracey, although there is a certain logical consistency. But if Brooke Manor is Baskerville Hall, the distance of over ten miles is too great for a late evening meeting in the Yew Alley. Within a half-mile west of Brooke Manor, however, is the crossroads hamlet of Combe, which is on what would have been the Yew Alley side of Sir Charles's home, and which is submitted as the real Coombe Tracey.

Holmes's Spartan residence in the moor would probably have been one of the prehistoric enclosed huts immediately below Huntingdon Warren, or by Hickaton Hill some three miles southwest of Brooke Manor.

For those canonical purists who may rightfully claim that Brooke Manor does not possess the magnitude of Baskerville Hall as described by Watson, there is still the Manor House at Moretonhampstead, which meets the physical and aesthetic requirements. It is not Baskerville Hall, but it beckons as if it were. But for those who take their Sherlock straight, Baskerville Hall is where it has always been, for three hundred years, since well before the time when Holmes and Watson graced its premises, at Brooke Manor near Holy Brook in West Buckfastleigh, hard by the eastern edge of Dartmoor.

Dinner in the informal dining room at Wooder Manor that night was a quiet affair. We were not Schliemann and Sophia, nor was Baskerville Hall Troy, but we knew how they must have felt. For me, my Sherlockian verities were affirmed, and for Audrey it was unsettling to find truth in what she had regarded as a joke. We both agreed over port and Stilton that we hoped that Sir Henry returned after his long, restorative sea voyage and, marrying the widow Stapleton, lived in peace and comfort under his ancestral roof.

XV. Cornwall and the Devil's Foot

WE left the Dartmoor area by train from Exeter to Truro on the same rail line which Holmes and Watson took in the adventure of *The Devil's Foot.* The London and South-Western railway was nationalized after the Second World War, but the road remains the same today.

From Truro, we drove a Godfrey Davis hired car which was waiting for us at the station. Motoring in England has its own peculiarities which the excellence of the maps fails to mitigate, such as the road signs. When invasion seemed imminent in World War II, all road signs were removed to confuse any invaders, but I am abidingly convinced that this could have been accomplished more effectively by leaving them up. In addition to the presence and absence of signs, the tourist must deal with their language: dual carriageways, town centres, roundabouts, and the reassuring STEADY. It was only after several driving trips that I realized the periodic GRIT signs were not encouragements to the insecure motorist but warnings of the presence of loose road gravel. The big problem, however, is the English insistence on driving on the left, which requires experience in judging distances right to left and in using the left hand to shift gears. While a car with an automatic transmission will avoid one problem, the other adventure is unavoidable but will result in making the acquaintance of many members of the English motoring public when you rake the sides of their cars. You must understand that the British are not always reserved. They drive fast, and the spirit of Morgan, Nelson and Drake is not dead but has been transferred to the highways.

Our own driving problems were augmented by Audrey the navigator's new interest in Holmes. After locating Baskerville Hall, her amused condescension at her husband's harmless folly had evaporated, and she was beginning to be a true believer. "We *found* Baskerville Hall," she kept repeating to herself. Her self-distraction resulted, as the locals put it, in several wrong turnings, but we followed their repeated advice to "press on" and did reach the bright green coastal hills. We crossed the River Fal on the King Harry Ferry with a proudly personalized KHF emblazoned on its smokestack. Our destination was the small resort of St. Mawes, a delightful village in the south of Cornwall, perched precariously along the side of the Falmouth Bay. This is the English Riviera, with an un-English scattering of palms warmed by the Gulf Stream. We had reservations at the Tresanton Hotel, which, like the town, ascends the hill irregularly. It is more vertical than horizontal but is a well-recognized bastion of solicitude and ease. Small by American standards, with only some 29 rooms, it regularly receives high marks from the most experienced travelers.

There is something indefinably unruly and unconquered about Cornwall. It is among the wettest areas in the U.K., which is no small feat, with rain and sea mist responsible for abundantly green vegetation in areas protected from the sea. Cornwall extends like a dagger into the vitals of the Atlantic, which in turn lashes it remorselessly. It is a rocky area, granite-hard, with an irregular, rocky coast deeply indented by the depredations of the sea. Man has long been here, as his barrows and tumuli testify, and Cornish tin was mined for bronze-age Phoenicians who sailed here regularly to trade for it. There remain none who still speak Cornish, a Celtic tongue akin to Welsh and Breton, but the language abounds in placenames throughout the county.

After a stalwart English dinner, exceptionally prepared by the Tresanton chefs, we had cosseted ourselves in our room overlooking Falmouth Bay. Slashing rain exhausted itself against our small windows. It was a fitting introduction to Cornish weather.

This began what might be termed Audrey's post-Baskerville phase, and she was interested in what had caused Holmes to come to Cornwall. I explained that his health had evidenced some danger signals as a consequence of his grinding professional exertions. After all, it was not an easy thing being the world's first consulting detective. Specifically, his physical condition had been aggravated by what Watson enigmatically characterized as "occasional indiscretions of his own." Upon the medical advice of an eminent Harley Street specialist, Watson and his patient found themselves in March of 1897 comfortably situated in a small whitewashed cottage on a grassy headland commanding a view of Mount's Bay, "near Poldhu Bay, at the further extremity of the Cornish peninsula."

I explained that there were three dwellings directly connected with *The Devil's Foot*: Holmes's cottage near Poldhu Bay, the rooms of Mortimer Tregennis in the vicarage, and the Tregennis home in Tredannick Wartha.

Watson is uncharacteristically specific in identifying the vicarage as Tredannick Wollas. The atlas shows a Tredannick in Cornwall which is, however, on the Bristol Channel side and is nowhere near Mount's Bay, which is also clearly identified and is on the opposite side of Cornwall. Poldhu

Poldhu Cove as Holmes must have known it

Bay is a recognized landmark, located on the eastern side of Mount's Bay.

The identification of the villages of Tredannick Wollas and Tredannick Wartha present more serious problems than that of the vacation cottage. There is no Tredannick Wollas in the area, although, as C. O. Merriman has observed, there is a farm called Predannack Wollas, which is a few miles from Poldhu Point. There is in the same area a Predannack Head recognized on the maps. There is no village of Tredannick Wartha (in which was located the Tregennis villa near the "old stone cross upon the moor"), but linguistics may be of some assistance. The *Oxford Universal Dictionary* states that "warth" means a shore or strand, or, in modern usage, a meadow near water or a coastal stretch. Predannack Wollas is near the coast, but not upon it, so that Predannack Wartha would have been between it and the coast. The prefix "Tre-" is of Cornish origin and denotes a farm or dwelling. It is a most common prefix in names of Cornish towns, and the family name Tregennis, containing the same prefix, establishes that the family was Cornish in origin.

We left St. Mawes the following day. The weather had abated somewhat, but the late September day was dour, with a fine rain fitfully whipped into what felt like stinging nettles by the sea-wind.

Poldhu Point is one of Cornwall's windswept, towering

Poldhu Cottage, now known as "Craig-a-Bella." Recent as it may appear in this photograph, it does date from the previous century.

promontories. Vegetation cowers close to the ground and survives the wind. The Poldhu Hotel, a Victorian structure which would have existed at the time of the Holmesian visit, continues to overlook Poldhu Bay, which would more accurately be described as a cove. Directly opposite, and to the north, on another steep cliff reachable by a narrow road snaking up from the cove, is a small whitewashed cottage, now unfortunately named "Craig-a-Bella." It meets all of Watson's strictures as being a "little whitewashed house, which stood high upon a grassy headland" above Mount's Bay. It is a one-story, rectangular structure with a steeply pitched roof, facing the bay, and across the front is a long veranda tucked under the roof. It is clearly a nineteenth-century structure. Standing alone as it does, it would have admirably suited Holmes and would have fulfilled his doctor's prescription. Its location, description, and age almost certainly merit its identification as Holmes's vacation cottage that spring of 1897.

The cottage is nondescript Victorian, and there are no trees around it, only tall grass, and behind it is a rather barren golf course. There is an attractive loneliness about the area which Holmes would have appreciated. The place is remarkably like the region on the south coast to which he ultimately retired.

That "independent gentleman" with the "foxy face" and "beady eyes," Mortimer Tregennis, had taken rooms at the vicarage in Tredannick Wollas, which is described as a "large, straggling house." The Tregennis quarters consisted of two rooms "which were in an angle by themselves, one above the other."

Tredannick Wollas was stated in the Canon to be the village nearest Holmes's cottage, and Mullion is the village. It

The vicarage at Tredannick Wollas possesses two rooms, "in an angle by themselves, the one above the other," precisely as described in *The Devil's Foot.* The ground floor room is not visible owing to the intervening wall.

is a pleasant rural market place of some three thousand people, clustered around the ancient, weathered stone church about a mile from Poldhu Bay.

The rain had increased in intensity, and it hurried our examination of the village. The Mullion vicarage is a two-story Regency structure, built of the whitewashed brick so popular here, and is pleasantly situated within walled grounds. It is rectangular in front, but it is attached to the parish house, and to the rear of and connected to each is a right-angled, two-story addition the right size for one room above the other. These rooms match the architectural description, and they could have been the quarters within which Mortimer Tregennis lived and appropriately expired.

As there was no one at either the vicarage or the attached parish house, I am unable to describe the interior of the putative Tregennis apartment. In point of fact, I was relieved. Although the British take their Holmes seriously, I was reluctant to suggest to the vicar's family that their quarters may once have housed a maniacal lodger. Britons cherish eccentricity and cheerfully tolerate grossly erratic behavior provided it does not harm animals or damage hedges, but even they would find Tregennis's manner of dispatching his kin quite unacceptable.

The Tregennis family villa at Tredannick Wartha is identified only as "a large and bright dwelling, rather a villa than a cottage, with a considerable garden," reached by a rural lane. This is insufficient data upon which to fix the location of the Tregennis villa, and its general type is seen throughout the Cornish coast.

To Holmes, it was "the Cornish horror—strangest case I have handled," and he was not given to overstatement. The tragedy visited upon the Tregennis siblings by the ministrations of the devil's foot fittingly occurred in the setting of wild and windswept Cornwall, and if an identification cannot be made as to the precise location of the vicarage or the Tregennis villa, their general location is known, and the ambience of the story remains intact today in tempestuous Cornwall.

At right: Groombridge Place, on the border between Sussex and Kent, identified by Conan Doyle himself as Birlstone Manor House

East Sussex

XVI.
Black Peter's Lair

It had been a good day. The sun made the South Downs a shining thing. It was a "butterfly day" as described by the Sussex natives. The wind and snowy rain of the day before were gone, and we had located what appeared to be Holmes's retirement cottage. We celebrated with that very British custom of cream tea at a small tea shop in the hamlet of Litlington. The thick cream is known as double cream, reminiscent of our American whipped cream. It is not put in the tea but on the tea cakes, above the butter and below the jam. Delightful, but hardly a substitute for a cold and companionable martini, a difficult thing to order in Europe, where the barman will bring you a glass of dry vermouth, room temperature.

We were comfortably settled in for another night at the Star Inn in Alfriston, a hostelry which began catering to thirteenth-century pilgrims on their way to Canterbury, the most holy of all English cities. Over a period of seven hundred years, one learns to serve the traveling public; in my case, the barman made a crisp martini. It was good to luxuriate by the large fireplace in the library, with its small windows and low, oak-beamed ceilings. There was the usual periodical reading fare—*Country Life, Punch,* the *Illustrated London News.* I was glancing at the latest issue of *Sussex Life* when that incantatory name Sherlock Holmes grabbed me.

Here was an article about the town of Forest Row, its

Brambletye Inn where it was asserted that Conan Doyle once lodged, and the claim that it was "featured in one of his Sherlock Holmes novels."

Forest Row was our destination the next day in the quest for the captain's cabin of Black Peter Carey, at Woodman's Lee, in which the bluebottles and flies buzzed like a harmonium about his harpooned body, literally transfixed against the wall.

Watson had placed Woodman's Lee near Forest Row. The erstwhile nemesis of Black Peter, John Hopley Neligan, stayed at the Brambletye Hotel, as did Inspector Hopkins, Holmes, and Watson. The canonical references to the Brambletye were few. It was in a village, a golf course was at the hotel nearby, and it was within walking distance of the Carey establishment.

Back in America, I had concluded that Gravetye Manor was Brambletye, based on a similarity of names and its location. Indeed, we had rooms booked there, and I had submitted a monograph to one of the Holmes societies making this identification.

Gravetye was the country estate of one of the foremost English landscape gardeners and is now one of the most elegant resort hotels. Its cuisine is so superior that the no smoking rule in the dining room is respected. It was within an acceptably Victorian walking distance, and as it had its own golf course it had seemed a likely Brambletye candidate.

The information in *Sussex Life* that there really was a Brambletye Hotel was too logical to be ignored and too providential not to be eerie. It was as if the massive shade of Conan Doyle had lent an ectoplasmic hand. Forest Row is some 24 miles from Alfriston and eight miles from Crowborough, where Doyle himself lived for most of the years of

The Brambletye Hotel. Despite its Tudor appurtenances, however, the building is of twentieth-century construction and probably takes its name from the establishment mentioned in *Black Peter* rather than the other way around. Note that the pub is called "Black Peter's Bar."

his second marriage. There are golf courses near Forest Row, including the Royal Ashdown Forest Golf Club, which was visited by Queen Victoria in 1889. A few miles north of Forest Row are the remains of the manor of Brambletye, and on the main street of the town is the Brambletye Hotel, a three-story, pseudo-Elizabethan structure of indeterminate age and undistinguished mien, replete with a Black Peter Bar.

Where was Woodman's Lee? There is no nearby village of that name, but Michael Harrison has suggested Coleman's Hatch, some three miles distant, reasoning that "coal" and "wood" are both fuels and "lee" and "hatch" are nautical terms.

Black Peter's home was "a long, low, stone house, approached by a curving drive running through the fields." It was situated in a clearing upon the green slope of a hill. Nearer to the road was the small outbuilding, with a window and door apparently facing the road, with the village outside Black Peter's gate.

Coleman's Hatch is a small village randomly spread over a hilly area, with no particular pattern or town centre.* At the edge of town, on Upper Parrock Road, there is a house which meets substantially all the requirements. It is stone, set upon its own grounds, with a long, curving drive. The house is on a clearing straddling the green slope of a hill, and, although it is two stories in height, it has the appearance of being long and low. It is called Upper Parrock House, and on the grounds between the house and the road, right where Watson said it was, is a wooden one-room cottage with a stone foundation, much like a captain's cabin—Black Peter's lair.

---

*For the reader of a more whimsical turn, A. A. Milne lived at nearby Crotchford Farm, and *Winnie-the-Pooh* was written there.

The view across the moat at Birlstone from the study, now the billiard room, in which the body of John Douglas lay. Upon the sill of this window was found the bloody footmark which was of such importance in clearing up the case.

XVII. Birlstone and the Valley of Fear

THE MANOR HOUSE OF BIRLSTONE, near Birlstone village, has the distinction of being one of the few scenes in the Holmesian saga which can be identified with certainty, although not unexpectedly several candidates have been advanced. To James Montgomery of Philadelphia, a member of the Baker Street Irregulars, goes the credit for the precise identification. He obtained a presentation copy of *The Valley of Fear* which Sir Arthur Conan Doyle had inscribed: "With all kind remembrance from Arthur Conan Doyle who hopes you have pleasant memories of Groombridge House which is the old house herein described. June 22/21."

The village of Groombridge is located approximately three miles from Tunbridge Wells, not the Watsonian ten to twelve miles, and is located in two counties, the New Town in Sussex and the Old Town in Kent. Groombridge House was, from the information available, still standing in the 1960s, and its owner was Mr. Walton Mountain. I did not wish to write to him if he were no longer the owner or no longer living, but correspondence with the local postmaster confirmed that he was alive and well and in Groombridge House. Mr. Mountain was not a Sherlockian, but he was tolerant of those who were, and a date was fixed to meet him and his house.

Watson had described the village of Birlstone as

a small and very ancient cluster of half-timbered cottages on the northern border of the county of Sussex. . . . It is the centre for a considerable area of country, since Tunbridge Wells, the nearest place of importance, is ten or twelve miles eastward, over the borders of Kent.

Birlstone Manor was of Jacobean brick, with many gables and diamond-paneled windows. Historically, there were double moats, but only the innermost, some forty feet in width, contained water. The only approach to the house was by means of a drawbridge which, significantly, was raised each evening.

Watson's descriptions of the village and the house are perceptive, and, except for the allusions to the distance from Tunbridge Wells and to the drawbridge, are accurate. Groombridge Manor House is situated in extensive, landscaped grounds hard by the river separating Kent and Sussex, dominating the flat alluvial lands formed ages ago by the river and protected by the sheltering hills. The entrance, by the parish church, is through a park, and surrounding the entrance to the house is a grove of immense and aged yew trees. Immediately beyond is the moat, with its permanent non-drawbridge.

Our host, Mr. Mountain, a quintessential English gentleman with the courtly presence of his eighty-plus years, received us in the English fashion. He had an evident taste for crusted port, and I was glad I'd directed Audrey in London to acquire a bottle of the same for him. He is a compact man with a generous enthusiasm in showing his home to appreciative strangers. The property is immaculately maintained, inside and out, with both gardeners and peacocks on the lawns. Beyond the jousting ground to the north and rear of the house is a working farm populated with the Southdown sheep which many years ago replaced the Jersey cattle which were the pride of Mr. Mountain's father.

The Mountain family purchased the estate in 1918 from the Saint family, whose head was for many years the appropriately named vicar of the parish, but the manor house was

The northernmost entrance at the rear of Birlstone Manor House. The "many gables" and "small diamond-paned windows" which Dr. Watson observed at the end of the 1880s are still there, and indeed the manor is "still much as the builder had left it in the early seventeenth century." The two windows to the left of the bridge are the only ones in the house which directly overlook the moat, and so one of them is necessarily the one upon which the detectives kept watch in the night. They open into the billiard room, which must be that used by John Douglas as his study, even though they are not "within a foot" of the surface of the water.

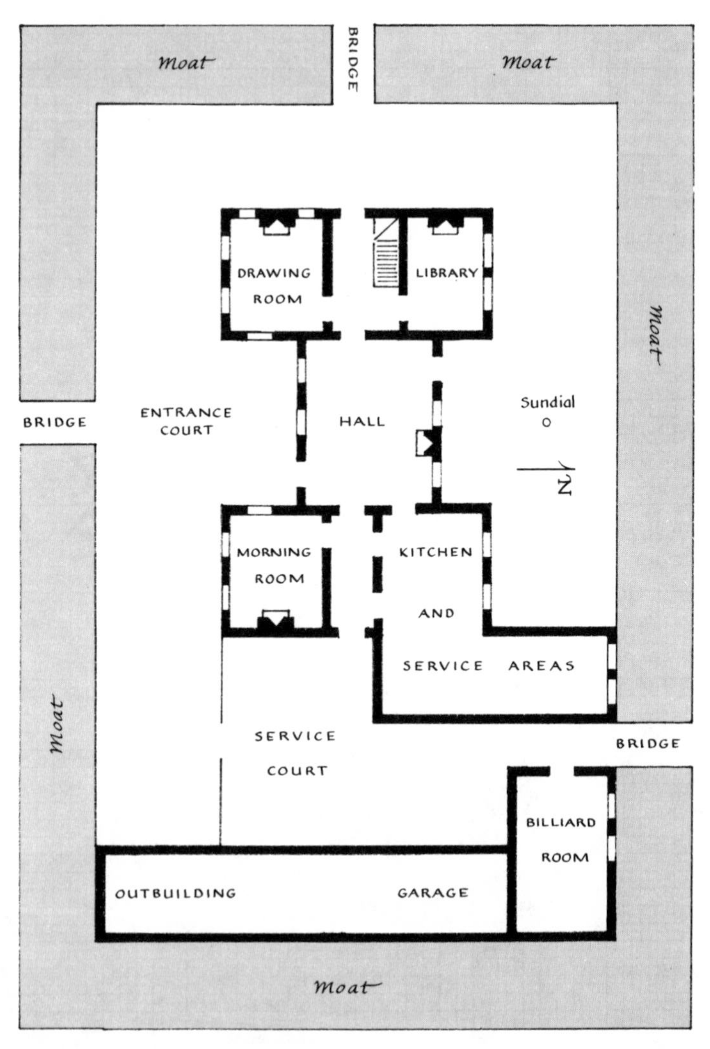

Plan of the ground floor of Birlstone, not to scale, showing the moat and the grounds within

built, not by the Saints, but by the Packer family, who had owned the land for over two hundred years. It was the Packers who rebuilt their pleasant seat within the confines of an older home. In the 1680s they built well but economically, the overmantel in the dining room being a bedstead and the foot of the bed appearing as a part of the wainscoting in the entrance hall. Watson correctly describes Birlstone as being constructed in the Jacobean period on the ruins of an earlier dwelling.

The Packer family portraits are still in the drawing room, and family tradition is that they emigrated to America and became Utah Mormons. There is a branch of the family still in Utah, who have visited the house—shades of Enoch Drebber, Jefferson Hope, and *A Study in Scarlet.*

John Evelyn, the celebrated seventeenth-century diarist, was one of the Packers' guests, and he celebrated his visit by planting one of the yew trees which now form the entrance to the mansion, but he wrote not wholly favorably of Groombridge Place.

Mr. Mountain is most insistent that Conan Doyle was never a guest on the premises in either his time or that of his father, a not unreasonable statement since *The Valley of Fear* was composed in 1914 and the Mountains did not occupy Groombridge until four years later. He does acknowledge that Doyle was once on the premises without an invitation and did, in a most ungentlemanly act, lure the house ghost, an ostler, into his automobile, which Mr. Mountain insists was the last time the ghostly ostler materialized. His gracious niece assured us privately, however, that the ghost did recognize its responsibilities and has returned. (Conan Doyle's own version of the incident appears in his book *The Edge of the Unknown,* published in 1930.) Mr. Mountain regards Doyle as an interloper, although he has accepted a dedicatory copy of Doyle's work from the Sherlock Holmes Society of London, who have visited the premises.

The house is authentically Jacobean, but there are not two moats, nor is the moat as wide as forty feet, and the ground windows are not within a foot of the moat's surface. Indeed, the only portion of the living area of the home hard by the moat is the billiard room, and it is apart from the house itself. Its window does not satisfy the one-foot test, however.

In the Canon, Inspector White Mason indicated to Holmes the window of the room in which John Douglas's body was found as being on the immediate right of the drawbridge as they stood at the front of the house, which would be the morning room. This would be to the south of the house, and the billiard room is on the north.

There are a sundial and Douglas's stone seat, which meet the canonical tests, and many other features which are not mentioned in the novel, including a jousting court (which delighted Audrey, who withal believes in knights and gnomes), an elegant formal garden, and an ambience which is thoroughly delightful. There are certain discrepancies in the canonical description which go beyond the vagaries of recollection. No doubt the changes were the result of a writer's inspiration seeking to sharpen and heighten.

Yet there is mystery about Groombridge Place: comfortable and pleasant within, it is solemn and forbidding without. It is not difficult to understand why Groombridge became Birlstone, and why the mystery here was "soon to engage the attention of all England."

XVIII.
Holmes's Retirement Villa

HOLMES had long savored his eventual retirement as the world's first consulting detective. He selected in advance the area and perhaps the place—the South Downs in East Sussex, overlooking the English Channel. There can be little doubt that his desultory Bohemian instincts, so carefully repulsed during an investigation, caused him to yearn for the opportunity to live quietly, simply, and solitarily. His essentially misanthropic instincts would not unnaturally lead him to the civilized mysteries of beekeeping, as would his logical and observational powers require that he organize his observations. What better rebuke to Watson's sensationalizing his cases than to publish his own researches on bee culture.

It was in September 1903, during the investigation into the strange, nocturnal adventures of Professor Presbury in *The Creeping Man,* that Holmes, disappointed at his professional efforts, advised Watson that it was "surely time that I disappeared into that little farm of my dreams." D. Martin Dakin concludes that Holmes retired that same month, and Watson explicitly states in his prefatory remarks to *The Creeping Man* that that case was "one of the very last cases handled by Holmes before his retirement from practice." "THE RETURN OF SHERLOCK HOLMES" was published in 1904, and Holmes had retired by then. There appears to be unanimity in the canonical chronologies that the retirement occurred between September 1903 and the end of that year.

Holmes's disposition was such that he fitted easily into a life of withdrawal and solitary contentment. It would require august persons and powerful arguments to persuade him to abandon his leisure, and indeed the Canon indicates the one momentous occasion when he did finally agree to return to practice. We know that the British Foreign Minister failed to budge him and that it was the Prime Minister himself who ultimately convinced him, each coming as a supplicant to his Sussex retirement cottage. He never advised Watson what blandishments were offered, but one would suspect that a baronetcy was hinted at, certainly the wrong bait for Holmes, who had already turned down a knighthood. His perception of his duty as a free-born Englishman was undoubtedly the deciding factor, as the problems were of Holmesian dimensions and the stake the survival of Britain itself.

Characteristically, what has not been resolved is the location of his rural retreat. Watson, with his customary zeal for geographical obfuscation, furnishes specific information which leads nowhere. In the preface to "HIS LAST BOW" there is reference to Holmes living for many years in "a small farm upon the downs, five miles from Eastbourne."

In his self-narrated adventure of *The Lion's Mane,* the Master states: "My villa is situated upon the southern slopes of the downs, commanding a great view of the Channel. At this point the coast-line is entirely of chalk cliffs, which can only be descended by a single, long, tortuous path, which is steep and slippery." His home is within walking distance, across the downs, from the village of Fulworth, which "lies in a hollow curving in a semicircle round the bay."

There is no village named Fulworth, so the points of reference must be Eastbourne and a town lying in a hollow whose configuration is in a semicircular curve around a bay.

EAST GRINSTEAD
Gravetye Manor.
FOREST ROW
TUNBRIDGE WELLS
GROOMBRIDGE
COLEMAN'S HATCH
ashdown forest
CROWBOROUGH
the weald
R.
Cuckmere
LEWES
SOUTH DOWNS
ALFRISTON
LITLINGTON
EASTDEAN
EASTBOURNE
BRIGHTON
NEWHAVEN
SEAFORD
CUCKMERE HAVEN
FRISTON
seven sisters
BIRLING GAP
Lighthouse
beachy head
cow's gap
Beachy Head Hotel

The villa is on the southern slope of the Downs, hard by steep chalk cliffs which are within walking distance of Fulworth and within a five-mile radius from Eastbourne.

Research quickly reveals that there have been four attempted locations of the retirement villa. Christopher Morley searched the area in 1953 and concluded that the cottage was approximately one and a half miles from the Channel and the same distance from the Seven Sisters, near a pine grove a quarter of a mile from a No. 12 bus stop on the road from Eastbourne to Brighton. Being a beekeeper himself, Morley reasoned that bees could not be kept in an unsheltered area by the cliffs. But as Holmes was most insistent upon accurate detail, it seems implausible that he would be in error about the proximity of his cottage to the cliffs, particularly in view of the several allusions to them in *The Lion's Mane*. Morley's offering accordingly appears to be too far inland to meet Holmes's own referents.

W. H. Chenhall opted for the area from the tip of Beachy Head near the lighthouse to the end of the slope west of Eastbourne where there is access to the beach at Cows' Gap. He recognizes that this region is substantially less than five miles from Eastbourne. Watson could certainly have been inexact in his estimate of the distance from Eastbourne; indeed, he may have even deliberately misstated the distance. Chenhall indicates a probable area, but he fails to pinpoint a specific location.

Charles O. Merriman opined that the cottage was at Birling Manor Farm, which is three-quarters of a mile away from Birling Gap but affords a Channel view from an adjoining field, and which farm keeps bees. Holmes, a most meticulous observer and scrupulous recorder, must have his words taken at face value, and he specifies a "great view of the

Birling Manor Farm, suggested by one authority as Holmes's retirement home, does have the proper look about it.

Channel." Moreover, the implications of Holmes's remarks, taken collectively, seem to indicate that the cottage was in close proximity to the cliffs and indeed on top of them. Birling Manor Farm, whatever its other merits, does not appear to meet these requirements.

W. S. Baring-Gould suggested that Fulworth is Cuckmere Haven. Cuckmere Haven is greater than five miles from Eastbourne, but Watson's accuracy may be questioned, and his motive may have been to preserve Holmes's privacy by means of judicious obfuscation. A more serious objection exists, however, in that Cuckmere Haven is not a town, nor has it ever been regarded as such. It is a small collection of buildings at the mouth of the Cuckmere River. While it does curl around that area, it is questionable whether Holmes would have characterized the mouth of a river, an estuary, as a bay. Reason indicates that we must look further for Fulworth.

Birling Gap, situated some two and a half miles east of Cuckmere Haven, has not been advanced as Fulworth. It is true that it is a very small settlement, and may with some justice not be considered a town, but it was an area to be investigated.

Spring in East Sussex in May 1979 was a strange time. While the uneasy confrontation of the Gulf Stream with the Arctic current in England results in fogs and frequent rain showers, snow in May is aberrational. It was in this weather, interspersed with the slashing of cold rain, that Audrey and I arrived at Birling Gap, which is at Beachy Head's western terminus. Today there remain an old hotel, a few cottages, and a rather large old building which may at one time have been used by the Coast Guard. It is situated clearly by a bay, and it is the only settlement from Eastbourne to the Cuckmere River. To proceed farther west takes one beyond the Downs.

A few hundred feet inland and northeast from the hotel, and at the base of the lowering cliffs, is the Birling Manor Farm house, an apparently deserted cottage with an obvious architectural provenance of the 1890s. It possesses the spectacular view of the Channel mentioned by Holmes and is precisely the requisite five miles from Eastbourne, as a nearby sign proclaims. While the cottage does afford a fine sea view, Holmes was most explicit that the cliffs could be descended only by a tortuous path, and at Birling Gap the headlands part to permit easy and level access to the sea. Moreover, the location does not agree with Holmes's statement that his home was on the bluffs. In addition, if Birling Gap is

Fulworth, the cottage is only a very few feet away and accordingly would do violence to the statement that Fulworth was within walking distance, as it is right there. If Cuckmere Haven is Fulworth, its location some two miles away would be a satisfactory walking distance.

Approximately one mile to the northeast along the Beachy Head road is another serious possibility. It is Hodcombe Farm, situated north of the road, a pretty place with farm outbuildings and a small grove to the west of the farmhouse. Bees could be cultivated here. The brow of Beachy Head is across the road to the south but at a sufficiently high location to block a commanding view of the Channel. A further objection to this site is that it is a working farm, and Holmes,

Beachy Head and its lighthouse. The steep chalk cliffs are precisely as described in *The Lion's Mane.*

with his precision of observation and description, would have described it as such if it were a farm, rather than his reference to a villa. It must be noted, however, that Watson does refer to Holmes's retirement domicile as being a small farm.

Because of the increasing violence of the cold rain, which reduced visibility to a few feet, we opted for the dry and warm comforts of the Star Inn at Alfriston. It was a Baker Street evening, with the wind cannonading the old inn, which creaked and groaned with the measured defiance of things ancient.

The next morning was more seasonable. Up with the wan English sun, I drove the short distance to the Downs, catching a glimpse of an early morning fox loping across the road. On

Holmes's retirement villa, just a few hundred yards from Beachy Head itself, is now a Natural History Centre.

The retirement cottage, with the Sussex Downs beyond. Its position by a small valley would protect Holmes's bees from the winds sweeping off the Downs.

this day, the search for the villa started from the opposite end of the Downs, at Eastbourne.

There are few buildings on the windswept, treeless South Downs. Gorse is the most prolific vegetation, but it is rarely shoulder high, necessarily directing its energies in the opposite direction to obtain a tenacious hold in the earth. The only road across Beachy Head is barely two lanes wide and runs roughly parallel to the cliffs. Few vehicles travel this out-of-the-way route from Eastbourne to Eastdean, which is more than double the distance of the direct route.

Just beyond the Beachy Head Hotel, where the road continues to curve to the south, and just east of and above the Beachy Head lighthouse, is one of the very few houses on the edge of the Downs between Birling Gap and Eastbourne. It is now the Natural History Centre, and its provenance is so far unexplored.

The house itself is a typical English cottage, one-story brick, high-roofed, and compact, nestling securely behind its low wall. There is a bow window in front and shutters on the windows. It is situated immediately south of the road, and the Downs swell upward gently for a few hundred feet to the cliffs themselves. The lighthouse is at their base and somewhat to the west.

Watson's descriptions are notoriously flexible, and the description of the farm at a distance of five miles from Eastbourne does not have the exactitude of the Master's words. A farm could reasonably be a cottage, and five miles could with equal legitimacy be approximately two miles, which the Natural History Centre is from Eastbourne. What we must not do is shortchange Holmes's own words. Consider an analysis of his description:

A villa. He does not describe it as a farm. A cottage, however, is not inconsistent with such a designation.

On the southern slope of the Downs. The cottage is clearly on the southern extremities of the Downs; indeed, it is on the cliffs themselves and within a few hundred feet of their edge.

Commands a great view of the Channel. The western exposure of the cottage affords just such a view. The cottage sits upon the chalk cliffs, and between the cottage and the cliffs is a monument commemorating the fact that it was at this point that Lloyds of London once received semaphore news signals and observed Channel ship traffic. The view therefore is demonstrably a "great" one.

The coast by the house is entirely of chalk cliffs. The site is

The view of the English Channel from the retirement villa is demonstrably a "great" one.

on the chalk cliffs and on the coast. The celebrated Seven Sisters are in the same area.

The cliffs are descendable by a narrow and precipitous path. The cliffs by the cottage may well have paths, and they certainly would be dangerous. What paths there were in 1907 might no longer exist, but also by the cottage is the notice that this is a Coast Guard "point," where volunteer lifesavers assemble when seagoing craft are in distress, which connotes access either here or at some nearby spot.

The village of Fulworth lies in a hollow, curving in a semicircle round the bay, and is within walking distance across the Downs. Eastbourne is the nearest town to the east across the Downs. It is only about one mile by walking directly across, but it is not, by even the most elastic stretching of the term, a village. The nearest town, again across the Downs, is Seaford, which is approximately seven miles by foot. While substantially smaller than Eastbourne, it is not within the definition of a village. Eastdean and Friston, while villages within walking distance, are not on the seacoast. Birling Gap is approximately two miles away across the Downs, and, as previously observed, it does lie in a hollow which could be legitimately described as a semicircle around a bay. The problem is that it now consists of a very few cottages, an unidentified building, and a resort hotel. It may well have been larger in 1907.

There is an additional and significant consideration. Holmes kept bees and wrote about them. The cottage must be in an area in which bees could flourish. Christopher Morley has observed that the winds on the Downs are not conducive to bees, but the area in front of and to the north of the putative Holmes cottage falls sharply into a large valley where farms are situated. Moreover, there is a sheltered area of gorse directly across the road from the cottage.

The Beachy Head cottage appears to meet all the indicia described by the Master. If this is not in fact that special cottage which housed Sherlock Holmes in his retirement, it does have special and significant claims, and beyond that there is a peculiar sense of appropriateness about it.

Epilogue

THE CHOICE of the term epilogue is deliberate. To have entitled the same "conclusion" would be the grossest presumption, as no one has the right to write a conclusion to the Holmes saga. It will go on and on so long as courage and intelligence and a sense of humanity are valued.

It has been the great good fortune of this writer to have explored much of England, itself a delight, seeking canonical sites. England in all seasons has an uncommon beauty, and even an English winter its compensations.

What has been the result?

Despite the frailties of recollection, the peculiarities of expression, the inexactitude of words, and the vagaries of time, there is solid and uncontroverible evidence that more than a simple majority of the canonical sites do exist. More than that, they exist substantially as described so many years ago by that greatly maligned gentleman-adventurer, John H. Watson.

But for those of us who cherish the Holmesian chronicles, it is not important that their accuracy be established. We are believers, and there shall always be a special part of our lives inextricably intermingled with Holmes and Watson. They are our good friends—indeed, if they are not our oldest, they certainly are our best friends. Their adventures are our adventures, as we are there beside them in their dogged investigations. The comfortable England of their day is ours also, and the fogs which too infrequently swirl down Baker Street also pleasantly engulf us. We need but a few minutes and a certain book.

To those who require the reassurance of visible places and tangible things to support their faith in the reality of the Canon, and to those who merely cherish the ambience of Sherlockian associations, this small volume has been respectfully tendered.

Selected Sherlockian
Bibliography

Baring-Gould, William S. *The Annotated Sherlock Holmes.* New York: Clarkson N. Potter, 1967

______. *Sherlock Holmes of Baker Street: A Life of the World's First Consulting Detective.* New York: Bramhall House, 1962

Carr, John Dickson. *The Life of Sir Arthur Conan Doyle.* New York: Harper, 1949

Dakin, D. Martin. *A Sherlock Holmes Commentary.* New York: Drake, 1972

Hall, Trevor H. *Sherlock Holmes: Ten Literary Studies.* New York: St. Martin's, 1969

Hardwick, Michael and Mollie. *The Sherlock Holmes Companion.* London: John Murray, 1962

Harrison, Michael. *In the Footsteps of Sherlock Holmes.* New York: Frederick Fell, 1960

______. *The London of Sherlock Holmes.* New York: Drake, 1974

______. *The World of Sherlock Holmes.* New York: Drake, 1973

Higham, Charles. *The Adventures of Conan Doyle.* London: Hamish Hamilton, 1976

Merriman, Charles O. *A Tourist Guide to the London of Sherlock Holmes* (reprinted from *The Sherlock Holmes Journal* 1970–73)

McQueen, Ian. *Sherlock Holmes Detected.* Newton Abbot: David and Charles, 1974

Starrett, Vincent. *The Private Life of Sherlock Holmes.* University of Chicago Press, 1960 (first published 1933)

Tracy, Jack. *The Encyclopaedia Sherlockiana.* New York: Avon, 1979

Illustration Credits

All illustrations in this book were photographed by the author, with the exceptions of the following:

Pages 17, 21: Westminster City Libraries

Page 33: From *Old and New London* by Walter Thornbury and Edward Walford (London: Cassell, Petter, Galpin), 1873–78

Page 39: From *The Charterhouse of London* by William F. Taylor (London: J. M. Dent), 1912

Page 45 (top): From the collection of Richard D. Lesh

Pages 45 (inset), 69: From the collection of John Bennett Shaw

Page 47: Whitbread & Co., Ltd.

Pages 49, 50, 63: Greater London Council

Page 51: From *Cassell's* magazine, October 1900

Page 52: From *A Pictorial and Descriptive Guide to London and Its Environs* (London: Ward, Lock), 1910

Illustration Credits

Page 55: From *Tallis's Illustrated London* by William Gapsey (London: John Tallis), 1851

Page 81: Drawn by William Luker, Jr. for *Kensington: Picturesque and Historical* by W. J. Loftie (London: Field and Tuer), 1888

Page 95: From *Rivers of Great Britain: The Thames from Source to Sea* (London: Cassell), 1891

Page 116: The Plough Inn

Page 133: From *Good Words,* 1886

Page 147: Drawn by Helen H. Hatton for *The English Illustrated Magazine,* June 1886

Page 159: Cambridgeshire County Council

Page 164: From the collection of E. F. Andrews

Page 167: Drawn by William Hyde for *The Victoria History of the County of Derby* edited by William Page (London: Archibald Constable), 1907

Page 181: From *My Devon Year* by Eden Phillpotts (London: Methuen), 1904

Page 183: Manor House Hotel

Pages 185, 193: Julie Hammer

Illustration Credits

Page 199: Drawn by C. Napier Hemy for *The English Illustrated Magazine*, April 1884

All the maps in this volume were drawn by Jack W. Tracy. Calligraphy by Mary Jane Gormley.

Index

Names printed in SMALL CAPITALS are canonical sites sought or identified in this book. A page number in bold type indicates an illustration. Italics indicate a map reference.

R. Severn
Gloucester
Cardiff
Bristol
Moreton
Hampstead
Exeter
Tavistock
Dartmoor
Plymouth
Truro
Falmouth
Mount's Bay
Mullion

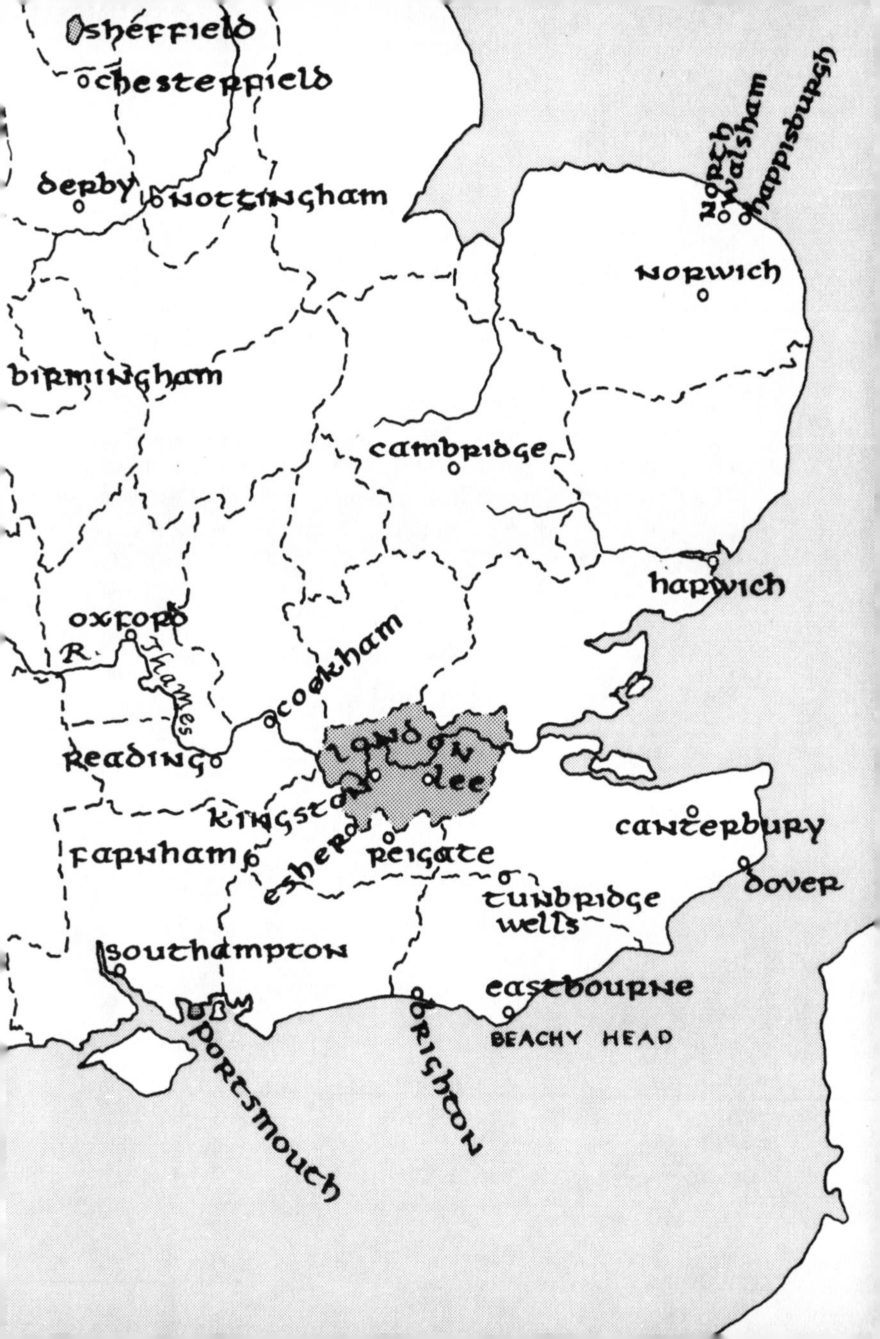

Sheffield
Chesterfield
North Walsham
Happisburgh
Derby
Nottingham
Norwich
Birmingham
Cambridge
Harwich
Oxford
R. Thames
Cookham
Reading
London
Lee
Kingston
Canterbury
Farnham
Esher
Reigate
Dover
Tunbridge Wells
Southampton
Eastbourne
Beachy Head
Portsmouth
Brighton

ABOUT THE AUTHOR

David L. Hammer is a prominent attorney of Dubuque, Iowa—but his lifelong passions have been travel and Sherlock Holmes. He is as intimately acquainted with the Holmesian Saga as he is with the byways of Vienna or Singapore, and it was inevitable that these two interests should be combined in *The Game Is Afoot,* a book of singular charm and authority about his favorite country and his favorite literary figure. David Hammer lives in Dubuque with his wife Audrey, lectures at Sherlockian gatherings, and is at work on both a novel and a second volume of travels through the world of Sherlock Holmes.